DEAR NEIGHBOR

REBECCA CASTLE

PROLOGUE

Dear Neighbor,

I don't know how to start this letter, I really don't. This is going to be really hard to write.

No, I'm lying...

This letter is practically impossible to write.

This letter is going to be the hardest thing I've ever tried to put down into words.

How do you begin to write down years of pain?

I certainly don't know how.

I have been sitting here at my stupid desk for literally an hour just trying to think of all the things I could say to you - all the explanations I could write on this piece of paper - but I have come up with absolutely nothing. Zilch. The stuff I've written down so far? I've simply thrown them in the trash. There's literally a pile of torn-up bits of paper right next to me right now. I've even bitten a pen because of how frustrated I've been, and now there's blue ink everywhere.

I don't know why I wrote that. It feels like something you would find funny. Something you could laugh at me about.

I wish I could make you laugh again. That's when I find you the most attractive. When your lips curl up and you snort in that super embarrassing way you do. I wish I could see that again. I wish I could hear you laugh again.

There's a lot I want to say to you, but every time I try to write it down there just simply aren't enough words in the English language to accurately describe what I'm thinking.

Believe me, this letter really is really, really impossible to write.

So. Fuck it. I'm just going to ramble on like this, and I'm just going to let all the words out in no order.

Here goes.

I know you didn't expect to see me last night. I certainly didn't. When I pictured you seeing me again, it was not in that way, with me standing there with the door open like that. I thought - somehow in my thick brain – that I would make it easy for you in some way, but clearly, I was wrong. Last night definitely did not go as I intended at all.

I know you want answers. It is completely fair that you do. I totally would if I was in your position. And, seeing as to how you reacted last night, I know there's a lot for me to explain. I know I'm going to have to do a lot of writing here to even come close to getting you to understand what's happened in the time since we've last seen each other.

There is a lot to tell you.

I know you don't trust me, and I don't expect you to, but what you're going to read written down here is the whole truth. Everything ripped from my soul.

My truth.

My explanation.

And maybe it's enough. Maybe it can help you. Maybe it can explain at least something.

There's never been anyone else. There has always only been you.

Let me confess...

PART 1

1

ABBY

Serenity was the first to spot the moving truck.

I heard the heavy vehicle pull up outside, but I was too busy zoning out in front of the TV to pay any attention. Even the crunching of thick wheels on gravel didn't rouse me from my potato-like existence in front of the screen. The show I was watching wasn't even interesting - just some cheesy Lifetime film - but I was too happy being a total sloth and mindlessly munching away on a bag of spicy Doritos to care what was going on outside.

It was only when my twelve-year-old sister scrambled from the couch and pressed her face hard against the window that I sat up and actually begun to take notice.

"Hey, look, Abby," Serenity called to me from the window. "There's a moving truck outside the Smith place."

My sister had a slight problem fully pronouncing her THs, preferring to replace them with a lispy F. I would usually stop and try to help correct her speech, but the news of a moving truck outside the old Smith residence made me quickly jump from the couch to join my sister at the window and forget all about her dodgy pronunciation.

I wanted to see this for myself.

"No way," I replied, following Serenity in pressing my nose against the glass to get a better look outside. "That place has been empty for like over a year. If it hasn't been bought by now, then no one's ever going to get it."

My sister pointed at the house next door in response.

"Well, someone's moving in."

Wow. She's right.

There was a moving truck outside the house next door.

I'll be damned. There is someone actually moving in.

And, judging from the large size of the vehicle being used to carry their stuff, our new neighbors were probably a family.

"I wonder who's bought the place," I mutter. The Smith house had seemed to be on sale for, like, an eternity. We'd watched different people come and view it over the course of the last year, but no buyers yet. Not until that day. My little sister's excitement was rubbing off on me and now I was super curious as to who the new homeowners would be.

"Let's guess who they are," Serenity said, flicking her hair back. She had it long and wavy, just like mine. She had always wanted to be just like me. And, with our same blue eyes and same dark brown hair, we practically were like twins. People always remarked that my sister was a little clone of me. Like my very own Mini Me from the Austin Powers films or something. "I bet they're just like us."

"Like us?"

"Yeah."

"What do you mean?"

"You know," my sister replied in her cute little singsong. "A girl my age who's just like me. I bet they're like us."

"Are you betting, or are you *wishing*?"

"But wouldn't it be cool to have a family just like us next door?" my sister asked. "Then we will have more friends. There'll be a girl like me for me to play with."

I chuckled. "And what about me? Anything for me?"

Serenity rolled her eyes. "Okay, there will be some girl for you to talk to about *boys* or whatever boring thing you want to talk about all day."

"Hey, that's not all I talk about."

My sister sighed. "No, maybe you can talk about *makeup* as well."

"Well," I replied. "I, for one, do not want our new neighbors to be like anything *close* to our family."

And I wasn't joking. The very last thing I would want was a replication of my so-called family. I turned my head back towards the hallway, towards my Mom's bedroom where she was doing God-knows-what.

No way would I want anyone to have a family like mine.

My sister, oblivious to my dark thoughts, began to jump up and down excitedly.

"There they are, there they are," she exclaimed, pointing at a car pulling up in front of the moving truck.

"I know," I replied. "I know, I can see them."

"I'm so excited."

"Me too."

My sister and I watched in rapt silence with our faces pressed up against the window as the car's front door opened. We held our breaths as we spied the people emerging from the car. They were a middle-aged couple, a tall man with a military-style buzz cut and a short woman that stepped out. I heard Serenity practically deflate next to me at the sight of them. I didn't know what she was expecting - or *heck*, what I was even expecting - but they weren't anyone remarkable at all.

Just a boring middle-aged couple.

But then the car's back door swung open, and out stepped *him*.

"Who's that?" I murmured under my breath as a young guy exited the back of the car. He was around the same age as me, eighteen. Tall, like over six feet. Skinny. With long straight blonde hair that pulled back over his ears. He slowly stepped out of the car and took a long look around the neighborhood. His face turned straight towards Serenity and me in the window. We both ducked down in a panic.

My heart rate jumped.

Has he seen us?

My sister laughed. "We're so silly," she said.

"Shut up," I jokingly replied, carefully checking back on the guy. He hadn't moved.

He hadn't noticed us.

Good.

I took him in, squinting my eyes to get a better look. He was wearing a black leather jacket. Dark blue jeans. His shoulders were slumped, and he had a general attitude about him of not giving a shit. I don't know if it was forced or natural.

I scoffed.

"He probably thinks he's a real James Dean type," I said to my sister.

"Who's James Dean?"

"Some famous actor from a billion years ago who a lot of boys try to be," I replied. "But I've never seen a single guy be successful."

Despite my immediate distaste for the boy next door, I had to admit that there was something *interesting* about him. Something mysterious. Maybe his attitude wasn't just some pose he was putting on, maybe he really did have that casual confidence and really did not give a fuck.

Or maybe he really was just a try-hard blowhard.

Serenity turned her gaze from him and up to me. "You like him," she said in a mocking warble.

"No."

"Yeah, you do. You *like* him."

I shook my head at my sister. "Shut up."

"I bet you're scared of him," she said, nudging me in the ribs.

I snorted. "I'm not scared of some guy."

"Yep, you are. I can see it on your face. You like him and you're scared of him"

"Nope.

"I bet you won't even talk to him, even if I dared you."

"Yeah?"

"*Yeah.*"

"Even if you dared me?"

"Yep."

Ha.

Screw Serenity.

Her big sister is braver than she thinks.

I stepped back from the window and stood up straight. "Fine then, I will."

"What?" My sister's face suddenly changed, realizing I was being serious. "I didn't dare you, though."

Now she was concerned for me?

"I'll talk to him," I said, taking a step towards the door. Serenity reached out to grab my hand.

"Don't," she softly pleaded.

"Nope. You said that I am scared of him. I'm not scared of some James Dean wannabe. I'm going to say hello."

"What if he's weird?" my sister asked.

"We're in broad daylight, Serenity, in front of his new house and his parents," I replied. "What can he possibly do to me?"

My sister whimpered, and I laughed.

"What if he has a knife?" she asked fearfully.

"You've been watching too many cop shows."

I took another step to the front door, unlocking it.

And then, as if he were waiting for this exact moment, my stepdad suddenly apparated by my side.

I thought he was in my Mom's bedroom. I thought he couldn't hear us or hear the front door opening. I thought I was safe from him.

I was wrong.

For God's sake.

The last thing I wanted to do was deal with my Mom's new husband.

Cameron nodded at the front door, at my hands around the handle. "Where are you going?" he asked. Out of the corner of my eye, I saw my sister sliding away from the window and back onto the couch, worried about the sudden appearance of our stepdad.

"I'm going outside," I replied, looking at my stepdad right between the eyes. He stared right back at me. I could smell alcohol on his breath.

"No, you're not."

"Yes, I am," I said, raising my voice defiantly. "I am eighteen and I can do whatever I want."

Cameron smiled. "Not under my roof, you can't."

"This isn't your roof, Cameron," I replied with a staccato emphasis on his name. "This is my dad's house."

"Well, he's gone."

Right then I wanted to scream into my stepdad's face. I wanted to scream that my dad wasn't gone. No, not just gone.

He was *dead*.

But instead, I didn't scream or fight back. I bit my lip and held my venom back. I was not ready to get into another argument with this man, especially not with my sister watching.

I felt Cameron's beady brown eyes flicker over my face. His horrible leathery skin was even worse close up. I wanted to get away from him. Fast.

"The minute I finish school," I told him. "The minute I do, I'm out of here."

"Good luck with that, honey."

I ignored him and opened the door. Surprisingly, he didn't stop me. He let me storm out of the house. I closed the door on him.

That was pretty tame compared to most of our interactions.

I shook my head, emptying the built-up tension, and headed across the yard towards the new neighbors.

They stopped and faced me.

"Hello, I'm Abby," I greeted them, offering my hand to the dad. He shook it with a firm grip. His back was stiff as a board, and he was immaculately groomed. So unlike his son.

"I'm Mr. Hunter," he replied.

Mr. Hunter? It was like he was treating me like a kid, making me call him by his last name like that.

I shook the hand of his wife, called Mrs. Hunter according to the dad.

No first names allowed in this family, apparently.

Then I turned to their son. To the smoldering James Dean-wannabe.

"This is Miles," Mr. Hunter said, gesturing to the jacket-wearing blonde.

I offered my hand to the guy, but he didn't even acknowledge it.

"Hi, Miles," I cheerily said, ignoring his attitude.

"Hey," he mumbled, eyes darting around. Never focusing on me.

That was it? A little slurred word in response? That was all he was bothered to give me?

He was so different from what I imagined up close. He was handsome. Tanned, smooth skin. A strong jawline. Bright blue eyes and full lips.

But my attention immediately turned to the space above his lip. A thin scar traced down from the side of his nose to his lips, only half an inch in length, but it was still very distinguishable.

A small scar that was *incredibly* hot.

My heart rate jumped again for the second time that day.

Miles Hunter was a beautiful man.

My new neighbor.

"Did you travel far?" I asked.

"A few hours," Mr. Hunter replied in his stern tone.

"So, you're new in town?"

"Yes, ma'am."

This family was very hard to talk to.

"I hope you settle in okay. It's a nice quiet street this."

"Thanks, ma'am."

"Any reason in particular why you decided to come here?" I asked.

The dad nodded. "My job relocated."

"Ah, right."

I pretended to ignore Miles, but I couldn't stop focusing on him in my periphery. He stood close to me, his hands in the pockets of his leather jacket, scowling at me. Unlike when I introduced myself to him, his entire focus was on me now. His eyes scanned me up and down. I didn't know what to make of him. I didn't know if he was disgusted at me or curious. Or both.

He was a mysterious guy, but I didn't want to give him

the time of day. He'd already been rude enough for my liking.

"Well, see you guys around," I said with a smile. "If you need anything, just knock on the door over there." I nodded at my house.

"We will," the dad replied stiffly.

I doubt he would ever want to talk to me again.

I gave them a little wave, and I got none in response. I turned around and skipped back towards the house, trying to blow Miles Hunter out of my mind. The guy thought he was cool. By the way he took me in with his eyes, he probably thought he was above me.

He was a gorgeous man, but not someone I would want to be friends with. His aloofness put me right off him immediately.

I stepped into my house and closed the door, feeling my heart rate return to normal.

Thankfully, my stepdad was gone, probably back in Mom's room. My sister was on the couch, pretending to watch that cheesy Lifetime movie, but I knew what she had just been doing. She had just been pressed up against the window watching me chat with the new family. She couldn't hide it.

Her little face spun around to me when I entered.

"What were they like?" she asked.

I shrugged. "Yeah. Fine."

"And that guy?"

"I don't care about him," I replied, dumping myself back to my regular spot on the couch and shoving my hand back into the bag of spicy Doritos. "He's just too cocky for his own good."

2

MILES

I took my seat at the table and stared down at my fork shining under the harsh lights of the living room.

Great.

Fucking great.

I thought I'd be able to get out of family dinner for once, seeing as we had literally only moved into the house a few hours earlier, but in typical Dad fashion, he had made us all sit around the new dinner table together. Pretending to be one big, happy family.

Ha.

That was a big lie.

It's tradition. That's what Dad had said.

But what tradition was it? Forcing your wife to cook up a storm even with half your stuff still sealed in moving boxes? That fucking tradition?

He knew that a family dinner pissed me off; that was the reason why he had forced us all to sit together like this.

He knew I didn't want to spend another moment in his presence. He intended to humiliate me.

And it was working.

"Help yourself to the peas," my Mom said, passing a bowl towards me. I took it from her and scattered a few onto my plate. I didn't intend to eat much tonight. I wanted this done and dusted quickly and to get back to my room as fast as I could.

"What do you say to your mother?" my dad asked me, looking at me with one eyebrow raised from across the table. His patronizing tone made my skin crawl.

"Thanks, Mom."

"Good," Dad replied. "I didn't raise you to disregard basic manners."

The more annoyed I got from him, the more powerful he seemed to grow. I hated it. I hated feeling like just some other teenage brat rebelling against their father, but I was smart enough to know that was exactly who I was. Just another mopey teenager forced to live under the same roof as their restrictive parents and moaning about it.

How cliché.

"Are you ready to start your new school tomorrow?" Dad asked me.

"Yep."

"You have all your things ready?"

"Yep."

"Your bag's packed?"

"Yep."

Dad raised a fork and pointed it towards me like a threat. "Because I don't want to go into your room and see that your new bedroom is a mess and that you haven't packed your school bag. You've had all afternoon to get ready."

"Yep."

"So, it *is* packed?"

I shrugged and looked down at my plate. I played around with my food, stabbing some mashed potato to avoid meeting my dad's glare. "I said yes."

My father's eyes narrowed. "Good," he said, turning the fork back to his food. I watched him stuff a pile of peas into his mouth. "Because this is your final chance, you know that?"

"I do."

"No more fights."

"Honey, maybe that's enough," my Mom interjected, patting my father on the arm as if to gently restrain him. "He understands."

Dad faced her, chewing on another load of peas. "I don't think he does. I don't think Miles understands the severity of the situation here for him or the fact that he has only two choices. This school is his last chance. It's the end of the line for him unless he wants to follow my path."

I didn't know what was worse, the way he talked about me as if I wasn't there or the way he talked about my *choices* as if I wasn't eighteen and couldn't make my own decisions in life.

"It's stupid for me to start a new school so late," I said, turning back to playing with my mash potato.

Dad straightened up in his chair. "Don't use language like that around your mother," he barked.

"It's true, though. What's the point of me starting so late? It'll be graduation in a few weeks."

"Do you want to enlist in the Army?"

"No."

"Well, you know very well that they're your only options. You either go to school and graduate, or you join the military. That's it. They're your two options."

The very last thing I wanted to do was join the military.

That's what my dad did when he was my age, and for my entire life he never stopped going on about it. To him, the Army was like a religion.

For him, there existed only two pathways in life: university or the military.

And I didn't care for either.

"I'll go to school," I replied.

"This is your last chance, or you will enlist just like I did. Understood?"

"Yes, sir." I sarcastically stressed the *sir* with a hiss of the *s*.

Dad really did not seem very pleased with that.

"Don't disrespect me at the dinner table, boy."

"I wasn't."

"I know what you're playing at."

Under the table, my hand curled into a tight fist. I was getting angry. Real angry. The kind of anger inside me that I was afraid of, the kind I knew I couldn't control.

The kind of anger that spurred me into proper physical violence. The same fighting that led me to change schools and cause my dad to threaten to forcefully enlist me in the Army.

That was it. I had enough sitting there around the dinner table playing *happy family*.

I dropped my fork on my plate and stood up. "This is ridiculous," I said. "I'm going to my room."

"Eat your food," Dad replied.

"I'm not hungry."

Before there was the chance for him to really lose his temper, I rushed out of the living room and into my new bedroom, slamming the door shut behind me. I locked it.

If I spent another minute around that dinner table with him, I knew I'd lose my shit. I was usually a very cool guy, but my dad knew exactly what the right buttons were to push to send me over the edge. I didn't want to lose control.

I really hated how he made me into that cliché rebellious teenager.

I stood in the middle of my bare room with the lights off. I was in darkness, just making out the outline of my bed against the wall and the moonlight streaming through my window.

I relaxed my hand, still formed into a fist from the dinner table. I hated feeling that anger again. The last time I'd felt that angry, I was punching the shit out of some punk who had insulted me. The guy deserved it, but because I was the big, tall one who'd dealt some serious damage, that meant I was the one to get the full brunt of punishment. Apparently, I was the *wild one*, even though the guy I'd beaten was the one who was insulting both me and the girl I was with. That was why I was kicked out of my last school. That's why I had to start a new one with only weeks left until graduation.

I took a step towards the glass and looked out across the yard, taking in a deep breath. I tried to calm myself. To not think about Dad. I glanced up at the half-moon above. It was bright tonight.

This was a quiet street.

I had to still unpack my moving boxes, but there wasn't much to take out, anyway. I didn't really care about having many material possessions, unlike a lot of teenagers I came across who were obsessed with phones and clothes and the latest gadgets. I didn't care for any of that shit.

I didn't really care for much at all.

I leaned against the window, my forehead against the cold glass.

I couldn't wait to escape. Get out of this house.

I really didn't want to start school the next day. I was never good in those environments. I could never fit in.

But, as Dad said, it was either school or the military.

I didn't know what I was even going to do after school. Maybe the Army *was* my best option. At least there was structure there. At least I could get away from here. Being on the front lines in Afghanistan surely was preferable to Dad's dinner table.

My eyes flickered over to the house opposite. A light was on in one of the windows. I could make out an outline of a girl walking around. I recognized her immediately.

It was that chick from earlier. The girl who introduced herself to us as we arrived, the one who bounded over the grass and offered me her hand like we were work colleagues or we were going to be friends or something.

Abby?

That was her name.

She was all cheer and smiles when she greeted us, but it felt like she was judging me the whole time. She spoke to my parents, but I could tell she was focused entirely on me. It felt like she was *appalled* by me or something. What did I do to her to make her judge me like that? Who was she to be on such a high horse?

She was cute, I could give her that. Pale skin, blue eyes, and long wavy brown locks.

Pretty.

My type of girl.

But I didn't like the way she looked at me when she came bouncing over.

Well, maybe if we were going to be neighbors, we should find out more about each other. I could clearly see her bedroom and the front door of her house from my window. It was only right that we spoke again. Maybe I might be able to find out why she didn't like me. I mean, there wasn't anything else to do on that boring street late at night. Only a few hours after moving into this new house and I was already bored enough to start picking on my neighbors.

I watched her from across the yard. She was working on something. Homework, perhaps? Her eyebrows were scrunched as she concentrated. Her lips formed into a slight pout.

Yep, she was really pretty.

I wasn't stalking her. She was the one with her window open and the light on. How could I not avoid staring at her soft face so illuminated only a few yards away from my own window? It was practically an invitation.

I took in her slim hands and the way she held a pen. There was something about her, something underneath. I kept watching her as she began to write in a notebook. There was something more to her than the sprightly neighbor who introduced herself earlier. There was something dark about her. Something sad.

I wondered what it'd be like to kiss those lips I was staring at. I wondered if she would kiss me back.

Maybe I should get to know the neighbors.

But first, to get out of this house. I lifted open my window and peeked over the edge. It wasn't far from the ground.

Perfect.

The window made it easy for me to jump out. Easy for me to get away from home.

Easy for me to make my way to the nearest liquor store and to persuade some guy with a few extra dollars to buy me alcohol.

It was my first day in a new town, about to start a new school the next morning.

And I had every reason to get drunk.

3

ABBY

"Do you want me to read you a bedtime story?"

Serenity scrunched up her little face at my question as if I had insulted her.

"Nope," she replied.

I gasped. "Why not?"

My sister rolled her eyes and shook her head. She was not in the mood for my games. "Abby, I'm *too* old for a bedtime story."

"Really?"

"Yes."

I picked up the Harry Potter book she was halfway through and dangled it in front of her increasingly irate face. "Not even a little chapter."

"*Yes.*"

I shrugged, placing the heavy book back down on her shelf. "I remember you used to love it when I read to you."

"Yeah, when I was five. I'm twelve now."

"Oh, a *big grown-up*, I see," I replied mockingly. "Sorry for trying to be a cool big sister."

Serenity poked her tongue out at me. I returned the gesture.

"I can read on my own," she said sternly.

She used to love me reading for her. I'd sit on her bed for ages, making her nod off to sleep.

What's that old stupid saying?

They grow up so fast.

Well, she definitely was.

I raised my hands and chuckled. "Okay, okay. I get it. I'll leave you alone, Serenity."

"Yes, please."

"Did you take your medicine?" I asked.

Serenity nodded to the pills on her shelf next to the Harry Potter book. "Yep."

"You did?"

"Yeah."

"You're not lying to me?"

"Nope."

I stepped out of her bedroom, pointing at the light switch. "You want it on or off?" I asked her.

"Off."

I flicked off her bedroom lights and slowly closed the door. "Goodnight, Serenity."

"Goodnight."

"Don't let the bedbugs bite."

And then, from the darkness of her room, I heard Serenity's tiny voice call out to me. "I love you, Abby."

It was so sincere. So sweet. So soft. My heart practically shattered into a million pieces.

"I love you too, sis."

I shut the door and closed my eyes.

Serenity and I loved to play-fight, but at the end of the day, we truly loved each other.

I took in a deep breath and headed down the hallway, back to my room.

On the way, I passed by Mom's room. I hadn't seen her all day, but I knew she was in there. Somewhere.

It really shouldn't have been me that was tucking Serenity into bed. It shouldn't have been me reading bedtime stories to her. It all really should've been our mother, but she'd been gone to us for nearly two years now. Sure, she was *physically* still in the house, but mentally, she'd clocked out a long time ago. Even before Dad's passing.

Now she spent her days on welfare. Drinking or shooting up drugs or whatever, I didn't want to know what she got up to in her room.

I wouldn't even care if it weren't for Serenity.

Everything I did was to protect my sister.

It was me who had to step up and be a surrogate mother to my sister. If my own Mom wasn't even interested in raising Serenity, then it would have to be me.

I walked straight past my Mom's bedroom and into my own, firmly closing the door as if to lock my mother and stepdad away. As if to close a portal from their world.

I couldn't wait to get out of that house. For a long time, I had resolved that the minute when school was over, I was going to get straight out of there. And I would bring Serenity along with me.

Just us two. Without the mother who didn't give a damn about us.

It would just be Serenity and me against the world.

In my room, I sat down at my desk and got my home-work sorted out for school the next day. I shuffled through the papers, making sure I'd done everything I needed to do.

All good.

I glanced over at the empty notebook lying on my book-case. Stupidly, I had made an impulse new year's resolution back in January to start a diary and I had yet to write a single word. I used to really love writing pen-to-paper, preferring it to typing. I used to always write letters. I loved the feel of the pen, seeing how neat I could make my hand-writing. It was like drawing or painting. Physically writing something always made me feel calm, and that's why I had wanted to start a diary.

But I hadn't got round to it.

I picked up the empty notebook and skimmed through it, looking doubtfully at all the pages full of lines. So much space to fill. Where would I even find the words? In a huff, I threw the thing back onto the bookcase.

Yep, I don't think I have the energy to start writing that anytime soon.

I leaned back in my chair and sighed.

And then I heard it.

Something was rustling outside my window.

Some kind of noise.

My head turned towards it.

The sound definitely wasn't the wind, or even some raccoon or wild animal. It was something else.

Something was tapping at my window.

My hands reached down below my desk to the baseball bat I kept for emergencies. My fingers wrapped around the rubber handle as I leaned further back to properly peek outside the glass.

A hand was there, tapping at the window. A human hand.

I made out a face on the other side of the glass.

Miles Hunter?

The new neighbor? The guy who thought he was so

cool in ignoring me earlier that day when I introduced myself to his family? That guy was tapping at *my* window?

He spotted me and stopped his tapping. I glared at him from across my room in disbelief.

And then he smiled.

* * *

"What the hell are you doing?"

I had to whisper to not wake anyone up, to not alert my family that I was outside the house, in the middle of the night, talking to some strange boy.

"I thought I'd come and say hello. Properly," he replied.

Miles Hunter smiled again at me, baring his perfect white teeth. He was still wearing his clothes from before. That black James Dean leather jacket. His tight denim jeans.

I wrapped my arms around my chest, fighting off the nighttime chill. I couldn't *believe* I had actually snuck outside to see why my new neighbor was tapping at my window. Maybe I should've brought my baseball bat. Maybe I should've been knocking him out to kingdom come for daring to make such a scene outside my window.

The last thing I wanted was for my sister to poke her head out her bedroom window to see this.

"Well. *Hello*, then," I said to him, making my irritation clear. "I'm surprised you're doing this. You weren't up to saying much when I met you earlier."

Miles tilted his head at my comment, as if he were confused. What was there for him to be confused about? He acted totally rude earlier in the day.

"I wasn't up for saying much?"

"It was pretty obvious."

"You were the one who ignored me," he replied.

"What?"

"I saw how you looked at me."

"And how did I look at you?"

Miles shrugged. "The same way you're looking at me now, with disgust."

"*Disgust?*"

Maybe he was right. Maybe my face did betray how I thought of him, but I wasn't *disgusted* by him. I just thought he was too cocky for his own good. The way he had mumbled at me and the way he carried himself seemed to me like he was nothing more than just an arrogant poser.

Up close, he was very different, though. Even more better looking than I remembered he was when I met him outside his new house. We stood outside my bedroom window, no more than a few feet apart. I could see him better now. The moonlight enhanced his strong features. His lips. His cheekbones. His blue eyes.

His scar.

I could smell him, too. He didn't have a strong stench of body odor or the cheap drug store deodorants that most eighteen-year-old boys I knew smelled of. His was of a light touch of aftershave. Something delicate. A softness that offset his tough masculine physicality.

And he was standing only a few feet in front of me. In front of my window.

"Why don't you like me?" Miles asked.

"Hang on, I never said I didn't."

"But you do think it."

I huffed. "I don't."

"Sure, you do," he said, taking a step forward so that we were getting real close. "You didn't like me the moment you set eyes on me."

I wanted to reply with something equally snarky, but

my thoughts were clouded by the realization that he was mere inches away from my body.

"I don't even know you," I stuttered, and Miles smiled again.

He was so confident with how he approached me. So flirty. So *sure* of himself.

He was so unlike any other teenage boy I'd known.

"Would you like to know me?" he asked.

I gulped. "Sure," I replied. "If we're going to be neighbors, then we should get to know each other."

This was beyond us being neighbors, though. And we both knew it. Neighbors don't stand only inches apart in the middle of the night. Certainly not like this. Whatever we were doing.

Flirting?

"Yes, let's get to know each other."

"If your window is practically opposite mine, then I guess we should."

"Exactly," Miles said. He reached inside his jacket pocket and pulled out a small bottle of a clear liquid, waving it towards me. "Drink?"

"What's in there?"

"Vodka. You want some?" he asked.

"No, thanks," I replied. "Wait, are you *drunk*?"

He nodded sheepishly. "A little bit."

"Is that what you do, get drunk and hang around neighbors' houses?"

"Only if I think they hate me."

"I don't hate you."

"Sure."

There was a long pause. Sensing that I really didn't want a drink, Miles carefully slid the bottle back into his pocket. Neither of us moved.

I needed to say something, *anything*, to break the extreme tension that existed between us.

"How did you get your scar?" I asked. I was going to point to it, but then I guessed that Miles would know exactly what I was talking about.

He smiled yet again. His scar flicked upwards when his full lips moved. "I got it fighting," he replied proudly. "You like it?"

That flustered me. "Yeah," I stammered.

Why did I say that? What is it about Miles Hunter that makes me confused in the head?

Why did I speak the truth?

Miles shuffled forward so that our faces were nearly touching. I sucked in air, my body refusing to retreat. It was like he had cast a spell over me. But, really, it wasn't anything supernatural.

I just didn't want to get away from him.

"You can touch it if you like," Miles said.

"Yeah?"

I felt his fingers wrap around my hand. Cold, soft fingers. He gently brought my hand up to his face and placed my thumb on the small, thin scar. My fingers accidentally brushed his thick lips, and something within my body shuddered.

It was like I was transfixed to the spot. Unable to move.

More like I was not *wanting* to move.

His face was smoother than I'd thought it would be. He guided my thumb over his scar, and I felt the bump of the skin where it was indented.

My heart beat faster.

I looked into his blue eyes. He focused on mine.

"You like it?" he asked again.

I couldn't even speak. It was like my throat had dried up.

I slowly nodded instead.

And then, in one move, Miles leaned forward and kissed me.

I didn't know what he was doing until it was too late, but I surrendered myself to the touch of his lips.

He enveloped me. I could taste him. He was soft and delicate with me, treating me like I was a lollipop to suck on.

It was the best kiss I'd had.

And then I could taste the alcohol on his breath. I could feel his arms wrapping around my waist.

And that was enough.

"Stop," I said, pushing him off me. Our lips broke apart and Miles took a step back.

He didn't say anything as I turned around and staggered back to my front door. I was so quick. I stepped inside my house and shut the door without a look back. I crept back to my room, careful not to make a sound until I closed my bedroom door.

I didn't dare hesitate for a moment. My retreat had been too swift for him to react.

I leaned against my bedroom door and steadied myself.

Had that really happened?

Had Miles Hunter *actually* just kissed me?

I checked out the window. My neighbor was gone. As if he had disappeared. As if he had never been outside my window in the first place. His house across the yard was dark. There were no signs of him anywhere.

I silently paced up and down my bedroom.

Why did I allow him to get so close to me?

Why did I say I liked his scar?

Why did I let him kiss me?

The minute I tasted the bitter flavor of vodka on his breath, I was out of there. No way was I going to get involved with some drunk, with some cocky guy who thought he was king of the world. I was not *easy*. I was not that type of girl who fumbled around in the back seats of cars with jocks.

I undressed, ready for bed. My head spun.

That was it. I was never going to see Miles Hunter again. I was not going to let him take advantage of me like that again. That was just going to be some weird one-off encounter I would forget about. He was just some drunk dude who was horny, and I was the nearest girl for him to annoy.

I wanted absolutely nothing to do with him.

But still, his kiss lingered in my mouth.

4

ABBY

I was busy trying to find my pen when Mrs. Winton, the History teacher, briskly walked into the classroom.

"Good morning, class," she said as she entered. I was digging around inside my bag to find the blue pen I was looking for, so I didn't get to see her as she walked into the room. "We have a new student joining us today."

My ears pricked up.

A new student? With only a few weeks until graduation?

Strange.

Finally finding my pen, I poked up from behind my desk, locking eyes with the new student Mrs. Winton had brought into the classroom.

And my entire body froze.

No. Freaking. Way.

"This is Miles Hunter," Mrs. Winton announced to the class, pointing to the boy with the scar above his lip standing in the doorway. "I know there are only a few weeks left of school, but I hope you all are welcoming."

Miles Hunter, the boy who drunkenly kissed me last night, was *in* my classroom.

Looking right at me.

He's joining our school?

Obviously, his family had just moved, so he would have to be getting his education somewhere, but I never even considered that he would be going to school, least of all *mine*.

But he was there, in the doorway of my history class, staring at me. And only me.

And I stared back.

"Hey," he mumbled toward the class. There were a few greetings in response.

I said nothing.

Please don't let him sit next to me. Please don't let him sit next to me. Please don't let him sit next to me.

"How about you sit at that desk next to Abby," Mrs. Winton said, pointing at me.

Fuck.

Miles turned to her. "Sure." His eyes flicked back to me. I didn't know what he was thinking. His face was completely blank.

But I knew he recognized me; that was as clear as day.

Maybe he was thinking the same. Maybe he didn't want to sit next to me. Maybe he wanted to avoid me as much as I wanted to avoid him.

But *no*. Miles didn't hesitate. He casually made his way towards the desk next to mine with all the cocky confidence in the world.

Fuck.

My eyes followed him across the room as he headed towards me.

He settled in the chair next to mine, leaning back with a sigh.

Right. Next. To. Me.

I was overwhelmed by how close he was, but I didn't want to show it. I tried to remain stony-faced. Pretend like he didn't exist.

"How about you help Miles, Abby?" Mrs. Winton asked. "Show him around the school. Induct him and catch him up on where we're at in History, is that alright?"

Did I even have a choice?

By the stern tone of my teacher's voice, I knew I was stuck. I knew I had to do this.

Triple fuck.

"Alright," I replied with absolutely zero enthusiasm. Mrs. Winton nodded, satisfied, and headed back to the whiteboard.

And I was freaking out inside.

I kept my head down, refusing to even acknowledge the boy next to me.

I was already formulating plans on how to do the least amount of this possible when Miles leaned over and whispered into my ear. "Thanks for *helping*. I'm going to be following you around."

Oh, he's really enjoying this, isn't he?

I turned to him. He was fully slouching back in his chair, grinning at me. Waiting for my response. My focus was drawn to his scar, but I redirected my anger at his bright blue eyes.

"Don't even think about it," I warned under my breath so that no one else could hear.

"So, you really don't like me?" Miles asked, still smiling. Still as irritating as he was the night before.

"I don't even *know* you."

"Funny. I would've thought we got to know each other

very well last night. I certainly did. I especially got to know your mouth."

I couldn't believe what he said to me. I wanted to rip his heart out.

But I didn't get the chance. Mrs. Winton had started talking. "Everyone, open up the new textbooks to the fifth page."

I bit my lip in surprise.

The new textbooks? *Crap*. We were ordered to buy them the week before, but I couldn't afford it. All my money went on Serenity's medication, and there was no way in hell I was going to ask for money from my mother, and even less likely she would give me any.

Buying a history textbook had been the last thing on my mind.

I raised my hand. "Sorry, Mrs. Winton, I don't have the textbook."

"You didn't buy it?"

Time to lie.

"I did, but there's been a problem with the delivery."

"Okay, fine. Borrow someone else's in the meantime," my teacher replied.

Miles raised his hand, copying me.

"She can read with me," he said loudly.

What?

"Perfect," Mrs. Winton replied. "Abby, share Miles' textbook until your one arrives."

Great.

Just what I needed.

Could this day get even worse?

I looked over at Miles. He was still grinning back at me, his lips even wider this time. He was *loving* this.

I scowled back.

I certainly wasn't.

* * *

My fingers span the lock around, finding the right combination for my locker.

"What do you think?" my best friend, Charlotte, asked me, leaning against the wall next to my locker. We were out in the middle of the school hallway between lessons, groups of students streaming around us, heading to their classrooms.

"Think about what?"

"The new boy."

I found the last digit on the lock. "What about him?" I asked.

Charlotte rolled her eyes at me like I was dumb. "You spent the whole class having to sit next to him, reading his textbook, talking to him. What's he like?"

Click.

I swung my locker open.

"I dunno," I replied, shrugging. I pulled out the notebook I used for History from my bag and slid it carefully into my locker.

Charlotte played with her blonde hair, twirling a strand between her fingers as she thought about Miles. "He's so... mysterious."

I laughed. "Do you have the hots for him, Charlotte?"

"*No.* I'm just saying. He's so... quiet. Unusual," she said. She eyed up a group of footballers passing by. Guys who would never speak to us. "All the boys around here are idiots, so it's interesting when some mysterious guy turns up with only a few weeks left of school."

"You really think he's mysterious?" I asked.

"He seems like he is."

"Well, he's definitely not," I replied, scanning my locker

for what I needed for the next lesson. "He's actually my new neighbor."

"What?"

"He's moved in next door to me."

"You mean *moved*, as in *house*?"

"What else would I mean by neighbor?"

Charlotte's mouth hung open. "No way. You never told me this."

I shook my head. "It only happened yesterday."

My friend paused and bit her lower lip, thinking.

"That's kinda hot," she eventually said.

"Shut up, Charlotte."

I was only going to keep the information there, no point in divulging to Charlotte about the midnight kiss Miles and I shared. I knew her too well. I knew she wouldn't be able to hold back from spreading that piece of juicy gossip around the school.

Last night he was drunk. That explained his actions. But in that History class he was sober, and yet he was still rude and arrogant towards me. It was humiliating having to sit there and read over his shoulder. I knew Miles enjoyed it, but I found every minute in that classroom painful. He didn't say much to me, he didn't have to. It was clear how much I found being so close to him uncomfortable.

But that kiss the night before, that was something else. I didn't know whether to relish it or hate it. But one thing was for sure: I despised the taste of alcohol in his mouth. That was what made me run away.

"Shit," I said, looking down at my bag.

"What is it?" Charlotte asked.

"I still have his history textbook," I replied, pulling the book out of my bag.

Great.

Charlotte looked over my shoulder, her eyes widening.

"What is it?" I asked her, turning around to see whatever it was she was staring at.

"Speak of the devil," my friend muttered, but I didn't need her to say what I was now seeing.

It was Miles Hunter.

And he was walking directly towards me.

5

MILES

THERE SHE WAS. Standing at her locker with my History textbook in her hands and with a shocked expression on her face. Staring right at me.

I approached Abby and her blonde friend, taking my time. They both seemed stuck to the spot at the sight of me swaggering over. I liked how I made them feel that way.

I liked to make an entrance.

"Hey," I said when I reached them, standing directly in front of my new neighbor.

"Hi," Abby replied, blinking blankly. My gaze instinctively fell upon her lips, the same lips I remembered tasting the night before. I'd been drunk, but no way in hell could I ever forget the soft touch of her mouth on mine. Never.

And then my gaze swiftly moved to her hands just below her perky breasts and my textbook clutched tightly in them.

"I believe that's mine," I said, pointing at the thick book held between her fingers.

Abby blinked again as if waking from a dream. "Oh, right," she mumbled. I noticed her friend smiling at me as Abby offered the textbook out. I ignored her friend. Abby was the only one I was after.

"Thanks," I said, reaching out to take the textbook off the beauty. As my hand took hold of the pages, our fingers grazed each other. Abby gasped at the touch, her cute mouth slightly opening in shock as our skin connected. I couldn't take my eyes off those smooth pink lips. Her hand felt the same as it did the night before, soft and warm. I liked it.

And then moments later, as if she was shaking out of a trance, Abby was back to normal. The familiar grumpy little face she loved pulling at me set in and I was back at the receiving end of her sass.

"Bye, Miles."

She started to turn her back to me, obviously trying her best to signal for me to *fuck off*.

But I wasn't going to go that easily.

"Wait," I said, placing my spare hand on her wrist. She glanced down at my grasp, annoyed. She was very cute when she was irate. I really liked how her small nostrils flared. "You have to show me around the school."

Abby furrowed her eyebrows like they were daggers at me. "No, I don't."

"Yes, you do."

Abby pulled her arm free from my hand. "No, I *really* don't have to do anything with you."

Out of the corner of my eye, I noticed her blonde friend watching on, a slight smile on her face as she enjoyed Abby and my bickering.

"Oh, yes you do," I replied to my neighbor. "Mrs. Winton said so. You have to show me around."

Abby shook her head. "Nope."

"You really want me to go and tell her you aren't cooperating? That you're leaving the new student out in the dark?"

Abby sighed and bit her lip, thinking. That really sent me over the edge. I felt my cock go stiff in my pants as I watched her teeth pinch her juicy bottom lip. I wished I could just lean over right there in the middle of the school hallway and kiss her. Take her as mine.

"Fine then," she replied after a moment's hesitation. "I'll give you the tour of the school. The *abridged* tour. Very shortened and very fast."

"As long as you're my tour guide, then anything's fine with me."

Abby turned to her friend. "You go ahead, Charlotte. I'll catch up. This won't take long."

Her friend winked at Abby before skipping off down the hallway.

"Bye, Charlotte," I said after her, knowing how much that'll annoy Abby.

My neighbor turned to me and huffed.

"Let's get this over with, shall we?"

* * *

"AND THIS, pretty obviously, is the sports field," Abby said, gesturing out over the running track.

"Obviously."

We stood by the bleachers observing the jocks run past us in their football uniforms as they headed out to train.

Abby clapped her hands together and smiled sarcastically. "Right, so that's everything. Am I free to go now?"

"Not yet."

Contrary to my expectations, Abby stayed true to her word and did show me around the grounds of the school.

The library, the toilets, the showers, the many different hallways. Kudos to her. It just made me believe that, underneath her veneer of sarcasm, she did actually want to spend time with me. That, deep down, maybe she did like me.

That she liked our kiss the night before.

"What do you mean, *not yet?*"

I smiled and reached for her hand again. This time, Abby didn't reject my touch. I pulled her towards the back of the bleachers, where no one else could see us. Where we could talk privately.

"You still need to catch me up on History," I whispered.

"Yeah, the history is that we're done, Miles." She glanced around where we were, realizing how alone we were. "Last night was ancient history."

"What's the famous saying?" I asked, still holding onto her hand. She still had yet to shake herself free from me. "History repeats itself?"

"Only if you don't learn from it," Abby replied.

"You're quick."

"When I have to fend off annoying boys."

"That stings. You find me annoying?"

"Yeah. The way you pretend to be so mysterious and such a bad boy. *That's* annoying."

I grinned. "You don't like that?"

Abby rolled her eyes. "No."

"Note taken."

She grumbled something inaudible. I liked how easy it was for me to wind her up.

"And anyway, why have you moved here in the last few weeks of school?" she asked. It was like she was accusing me of something. "Why bother?"

I shrugged. "I have to graduate somehow."

"Yeah, but why move now? Did you get kicked out of your old school? Expelled?"

"Something like that."

Abby nodded, smug and self-satisfied that she'd got to the root of my reason for being there at her school. It was no secret, though. I had nothing to hide. Not from her.

"What was it that got you kicked out?" she asked. "You kissed a girl you weren't supposed to or something?"

I took in a deep breath. "I got into a fight."

Abby snorted derisively. "Righto. You were drunk, I presume?"

"No. The guy was insulting a girl I was on a date with."

Abby's top lip quivered. "A date?"

"We're not together, if that's what you mean," I replied quietly. "The guy insulted the girl and so I had to give him the justice he deserved."

"So, that's who you are? A *vigilante*?" Her tone was mocking, but I sensed the admiration underneath.

"Yeah. Like Batman."

"Oh god."

"Do you like picturing me that way?" I asked, taking a step towards her.

"I don't give a damn," Abby replied, but her heart was not in it. It was the weakest sentence I'd heard coming from her pretty mouth.

Underneath the bleachers by the sports field, it was just like the night before. The same kind of electricity existed between us and we both knew it. I saw the flash of recognition in Abby's eyes. It was just like those charged and thrilling moments before we kissed in the dark outside her window.

I pulled her even closer towards me with the fingers around her wrist, and with my spare hand, I reached out and held her warm cheek. She didn't resist. Just like when our hands grazed earlier under the textbook, Abby gasped.

Her mouth slightly opened just like before, in that incredibly sexy way that made my cock hard.

We were truly alone there under the bleachers. No one could see us, even though we were surrounded by students all around.

It made it seem dangerous.

Exciting.

Taboo.

"I want to kiss you, Abby."

My hushed words sparked something in her. She whimpered at the sound of my voice.

But then she spun away, flicking her hand from my grasp and shaking her head free from my fingers. She was back to sassy old Abby, the one who glared at me as I sat next to her in History class.

"Last night was stupid," she said in a loud voice. "Don't you get any ideas, Miles. I am never, *ever* going to kiss you again, you understand?"

Without giving me a chance to respond, she began marching away back to the school hallways.

She was gone, just like the night before.

"We'll see," I called out after her. She didn't react to my words. She carried on stamping away, but I knew she heard me.

I knew she wanted to kiss me.

It would only be a matter of time.

6

ABBY

I LEANED over and waved the medication container at Serenity; the pills rattling inside.

"Have you taken them today?" I asked my sister, frowning.

Sitting on her bed, she pouted back at me. "Yes."

I raised my eyebrows at my sister. I knew when she was lying. I knew her too well. "*Really?*"

Sensing I'd found her out, Serenity puffed her cheeks out and shook her head. "Not yet."

"Great."

"But I was planning to."

"You know what happens when you don't take them," I said. "You know how serious it can be."

"I know."

"You have to take this seriously."

"I am."

"Really seriously."

"I do."

I slowly threw the container towards her. Serenity caught it with one hand, staring down at the pills glumly. "Take them," I commanded sternly. "Before I force them down you."

"Okay," Serenity quietly replied, resigned. "They taste horrible, though. I hate swallowing pills."

"It's either take them or hospital," I said. I reached over and handed my sister a glass of water.

"I know." She popped two pills into her mouth and gulped them down with the drink.

"There," I said. "That wasn't too hard, was it?"

"Easy for you to say. You don't have to take them every day."

I sighed and sat down beside her on the bed. I ran a hand through her smooth hair. "You know I don't mean to lecture you, Serenity," I whispered gently. "I only want what's best for you."

She nodded and pulled herself in close to me, wrapping her arms around my waist and resting her head on my shoulder.

I hated having to act as a mom to my own sister. I hated having to tell her off. I hated spending every minute of the day worried about her medical conditions and making sure she took her pills on time.

We sat there on her bed in her room for the next few minutes in comfortable silence. Just us two. Me stroking her hair and Serenity resting against my body in a state of peace.

Those were the moments I lived for.

"Right," I announced, standing up. "I have to get ready for work."

"Do you really have to go?" my sister asked.

I pointed at the pill container in her hand. "Someone has to pay for those."

She rolled her eyes at me and lay back in her bed, watching me as I got dressed in my work uniform. She giggled at how ugly it was. I couldn't argue; the cheesy corporate uniform was a disgusting sight. It would've been better if I'd served coffees in my bra and panties rather than the brown and yellow monstrosity that was the regulated franchise uniform.

I clipped the buttons together.

Yeah, what an ugly uniform.

"The new neighbor?" my sister asked. "What's his name?"

I twirled around to her. "Who're you talking about?"

But I knew *exactly* who she was talking about.

"The guy in the leather jacket?"

I chuckled. "Oh, *him*. Miles Hunter."

"Right."

I tilted my head. "Why do you ask?"

Serenity glanced down at her nails, picking at them. "Nothing."

"Really? What's happened?"

My sister waved her arm as if what she said didn't mean anything. "I just saw him earlier, that's all."

"Okay."

I wasn't buying it.

"On the street."

"That's all?"

"Yep, that's all," she said.

I eyed her suspiciously. Maybe my little sister had developed some kind of schoolgirl crush on the bastard. "He's in my class at school," I told her.

Her eyes widened. "Really? What's he like?"

Oh, I see now, her coyness has pretty abruptly changed to excited curiosity?

First Charlotte and now my sister. It seemed like Miles Hunter inspired that kind of attraction in women.

And I can see why.

"He's an asshole," I replied, and Serenity laughed at my insult.

"How?"

"He just is."

I thought back on that afternoon, and on my little tour of the school for him. The way he gently held my arm and guided me into the secret alcove under the bleachers so that we were alone. The tender way he touched my face. His pure confidence in thinking I would just bend to his will and give him another kiss right there next to the sports field.

No way.

No way was I going to give in to him, no matter how alluring I found his scar and his mysterious background, or the cocky and sexy way he spoke to me. I knew enough to know that boys like Miles Hunter meant only one thing. *Trouble.*

And I already had enough on my plate as it was with school, work, and my sister's health to even begin to contemplate dealing with troublesome boys.

It was best just to forget about him. Put my head down, get through my last few painful weeks before graduation, and then fly on out of there.

Forget Miles Hunter. Forget my new neighbor.

My sister went silent, thinking about what I said about that guy. I paid her no attention and finished readying myself for work.

I stood in front of her mirror and adjusted my ugly work top. I tied my hair into a ponytail and made a face at myself in the mirror, making my sister giggle again.

"Time to serve some annoying people," I said, winking at Serenity.

The door to my sister's bedroom suddenly swung open, and in stepped Mom.

I turned to look at her.

Here we go.

It had been a couple of days since I last saw her, and this time she looked even worse than the last. Her hair was a mess. She wasn't wearing any makeup. Her skin seemed like it hadn't seen sunlight for weeks. Her eyes were sunken into two dark pits.

"Hello," she whispered.

"Hi, Mom," I said, squaring my shoulders with her. My breathing went shallow, and I felt adrenaline course through my veins. I hated how seeing my mother always meant something bad.

And this time was no different.

"You're going to work?" she asked me, her voice raspy. My sister sat up in bed behind me.

I had to be strong. For her. She shouldn't have to see her own Mom in such a state as this. I had to keep the peace. There was no need for screaming and yelling. Not in front of Serenity.

"I am," I replied. "I'm actually about to head off now."

"You're working quite a lot."

I nodded. "I have to. Serenity's medication is expensive."

Mom ignored that last statement. "You couldn't spare a few dollars?" she asked, reaching out with her bony hand.

"I can't, Mom. Sorry."

"Really? But you're working a lot. I see you skip off down the street every day."

"All my money goes on school supplies or Serenity's pills," I replied. "I have no savings."

"Not even ten bucks?"

I shook my head. It was wrong for Mom to ask for

money like this in front of Serenity. It wasn't fair on my sister to have to witness this.

"I can't."

Above Mom's shoulder, the familiar face of my Stepdad peered into view. He glared at me. "Give your mother a few bucks," he snarled. "I'm sure you can spare them."

"I really can't, and I really have to get to work."

"You're really going to let your Mom go hungry?"

"There's food in the fridge," I replied to my stepdad. "And if you need more money for drugs, I'm sure you can speak to your welfare officer."

That threw him over the edge.

"You're such a little bitch," Cameron barked. "You know that?"

Just what I expected from him.

"Thanks for that."

"It's true."

I looked at my mother, but she didn't even have the will to match my eye contact.

"You're going to let him say that kind of stuff to your daughter?"

Mom said nothing.

"Hand over the money," Cameron said. "*Bitch.*"

I brushed past Mom to make my way out of Serenity's room and towards the front door of the house. "I can't wait till I'm out of here in just a few weeks," I grumbled. "And I'm taking my sister with me."

Cameron followed me. "Good luck with that, girl. Good luck finding a way to get her off us."

"Oh, I will. Watch me."

Cameron growled like a dog as I marched away down the hallway. "I can't wait for you to leave my house," he called after me.

"As I keep saying, it's Dad's house."

"And he's dead."

I burst out of the front door, refusing to let my stepdad see my face.

If he did, he'd have seen the tears streaming down my cheeks.

I left that house and sprinted down the street until the place was no longer in view. Until I felt like I was safely out of sight of my stepdad.

I didn't stop crying until I made it to work.

7

ABBY

THE DESK next to mine was empty when History class began, and it made me nervous. Fidgety.

All because of one boy who wasn't there.

I knew I shouldn't have been thinking about Miles Hunter, that I should've just forgotten about the asshole, but I did feel a pang of sadness when he didn't even turn up for History class. As I sat there, with Mrs. Winton strolling in and opening the lesson, I couldn't help running through the reasons in my mind as to why he hadn't shown up that day.

Maybe he'd always planned to only turn up for one day of school and then disappear. Maybe he'd been expelled just like what had happened at his old school. Maybe he'd gotten into another fight. Maybe he'd found some other girl willing enough to screw him underneath the bleachers, and that was where he was currently.

Or maybe he just didn't like me and didn't want to spend a whole class sitting next to me.

Damn.

Why did I go sad at that thought? I really shouldn't have been thinking about Miles.

He was a flirty bad boy.

Not what I was after at all. I shouldn't get involved with someone like him.

And yet he had a hold over my mind. I couldn't get him out of my thoughts, so much so that I was so wrapped up in my daydreams about him that I didn't even hear Mrs. Winton calling out my name until she was standing over me with an outraged look on her face.

"Miss Starr?"

Shit.

"Yes?"

The History teacher's glasses slid down to the tip of her nose as she leaned over me. "Did you hear what I said?" she asked.

And I knew then I was done for.

"Um... no."

Mrs. Winton scowled. I felt the rest of the class' eyes on me as I shifted uncomfortably in my seat. The teacher leaned over me and muttered. "Open your textbook to page 20."

Oh.

The textbook.

Shit.

It was nonexistent.

Before I could tell her I still didn't have one, the door behind Mrs. Winton slammed open, and into the classroom stepped Miles Hunter.

There he is.

The teacher snapped her head at him. He drew all the attention away from me.

Of course he did. How could anyone resist his mysterious aura?

"You're late, Mr. Hunter," the teacher said, completely forgetting about me. I breathed a sigh of relief, but whether that was suddenly being let off the hook for my textbook or for the relief that Miles was back in my life, I didn't know. And that terrified me.

At least he's here.

At least he made everyone disregard me and my invisible textbook. That was a plus.

Miles shrugged his shoulders. "Whoops," he mumbled back in response to the teacher. Mrs. Winton glowered at him.

"Fine," she said, clearly realizing that getting annoyed at him was a pointless battle. A realization I'd also had. "Take your seat and make sure that doesn't happen again."

Miles skipped past her as she returned to her place in front of the whiteboard at the top of the class. He headed straight for his desk next to mine, giving me a cheeky wink as he sat.

My body stiffened and my throat caught when he acknowledged me.

I couldn't focus on what Mrs. Winton was saying at the front of the class, with Miles now sitting so close. His presence dominated my mind.

I could barely even breathe.

As the History teacher rambled on about the economic effects of the end of the Civil War, I spotted Miles leaning over towards me. I felt his hot breath on my neck as his hand reached under my desk to tug at my sleeve.

"Hey," he whispered. "Abby."

"What?"

I spoke quickly and hushed so that Mrs. Winton

wouldn't hear. I didn't want to get into trouble for a second time that lesson, especially not on account of Miles Hunter.

"Here," my neighbor said, tugging at my sleeve again. Before I could react, I felt something being pushed into my hand. Something thick and heavy.

Something covered in wrapping paper.

A present?

I froze.

Miles had slid over a present into my hand, but why? What was he doing giving me a gift?

I took a hold of it and tightly clutched it in my hands. Miles pulled away from me and leaned back into his chair in his usual cocky slouching style, as if nothing had occurred.

But my heart was racing.

I couldn't open the present. Not there. Not in that quiet class whilst Mrs. Winton spoke.

The thing in my hands was definitely weighty. Long and chunky, but still bendable.

What even is this?

Not knowing what to do with it, I quietly unzipped my bag underneath my desk and fitted the present in there. For after class.

If Miles was watching me do that, he didn't show it.

We didn't speak for the rest of the lesson. We didn't even make eye contact.

And, when the bell finally rang for the end of the class, Miles disappeared as quickly as he arrived, gone out of the room with the flow of students.

It took me a moment to calm myself down and compose myself. My eyes darted back to my bag, to the present inside.

What the hell did he give me?

* * *

I SCANNED the rows of books, trying to find the perfect aisle to hide in.

Found it.

This part of the school library was devoid of students. Devoid of any noise and roaming kids that could look over my shoulder. I darted down the aisle and sat down against the wall, dropping my school bag in front of me and reaching in for Miles' present.

I hadn't opened it yet; I was afraid of revealing its contents - whatever they were - to a busy school hallway full of students.

But here, in the warm quiet of the empty library, I was safe to see what the hell Miles had given me.

For the rest of the class, my heart had been beating extra fast as I thought of what it could be.

I honestly didn't know.

Why had he given me a present?

If the point of his little stunt was to freak me out, then Miles had done a remarkable job of it. I was *really* freaking out by the time I reached the library. I needed to know what it was.

I took a deep breath and pulled out the gift from my bag. I was correct back in the classroom; it was covered in wrapping paper. A light blue.

Just like the color of his eyes.

Stop it, Abby. I shouldn't be overthinking this.

It didn't seem to be anything dangerous. What kind of surprises could he have hidden under there?

I tore away at the packaging, revealing the present underneath.

It didn't take me more than a second to realize what he'd gotten me. I gasped when I saw it.

A history textbook.

It looked like a brand-new copy.

I stifled a snort. Of course. What a joke.

But I had to admit, it was kinda funny.

"Screw you, Miles," I whispered under my breath.

As I inspected the book, a slip of paper fell from its pages and onto the floor.

Huh.

I picked it up.

A letter.

Handwritten.

It must've been for me. He must've slipped it in the front pages for me to find.

Well, in for a penny, in for a pound. I just had to read it now.

I unfolded the paper and started to read.

Dear Neighbor,

If you're reading this, then that means you gave into temptation and opened my present. That's a win for me, I guess.

I hope you enjoy reading about ancient history. There's probably an entry in the textbook about that kiss we shared the other night. I know that, for me, it was pretty world-changing. To you, it might be ancient history, but for me, it was only the beginning of the future.

Look, I know you were lying yesterday in class when you said you were still waiting for your own textbook to be delivered. I saw right through you, even if the teacher didn't. I know you, Abby Starr. Whatever the reason is for you to not have a stupid textbook, I hope this makes a fine substitute.

And now, back to that kiss. I'm sorry if you feel like I pushed you too hard, or if you felt I was too drunk. I wasn't too drunk to know I would want to repeat that kiss a million times more. But if you truly want me to back away, then I shall.

Or if you want to repay me for getting you this textbook, how about you do what the teacher asked you to do and help catch me up on History?

We are neighbors, after all.

THERE WAS NO SIGNATURE, but there was no point in having one. I knew it was Miles. He was so beautifully annoying, even in letter form.

His handwriting was far neater than what I would expect from such a boy. Tidy and cursive. I liked it.

Maybe he wrote a lot of letters.

Maybe he wrote a lot of letters to a lot of girls.

But I still couldn't help my body shuddering at his words. *I would want to repeat that kiss a million times more.*

Damn. The guy knew how to hit me in the heart.

When I finished reading it for the first time, I immediately did it again. I wanted to soak in his words, relish in his tight handwriting.

The more I read it, the more I understood how revealing and vulnerable the letter was. How Miles really put himself on the line writing it to me, a girl he'd only met a few days ago. He was so sure of himself. So forward. He knew exactly what he wanted and didn't flinch away from it. So unlike all the other idiotic guys his age.

The letter made my head spiral.

Maybe he wasn't just a drunk wannabe bad boy, maybe he was capable of more. Maybe there was more to him underneath the surface.

Damn, Abby. You made a promise to yourself last night before work to forget about him and yet here you are, in a corner of the library, sweating over the writings of your new neighbor.

It was hard to ignore the fact that, like a fish, he'd caught my interest hook, line, and sinker.

Fuck.

I didn't see Miles for the rest of the school day, and it wasn't for lack of trying. I was constantly scanning the school hallways and classrooms as I walked past, searching for his face. For his blue eyes. For his long blonde hair. For his thin scar.

But I couldn't find him.

When the bells for the end of the day rang, I rushed home. I had a very limited amount of time between school and when I had to start work, but I had a lot of things to do.

One very important thing to do.

The first thing I did when I arrived home was to sit at my bedroom desk, take out a pen and piece of paper, and start writing a letter.

8

MILES

I stood at my bedroom window and stared across the yard at Abby's front door. My new room was perfectly situated to look into both her own bedroom and her front driveway. It was perfect for me.

All I wanted to do right then was to jump over the fence separating us both, take her in my arms, and kiss her. But I could not. She'd told me she didn't want to kiss again, and I was going to respect her wishes.

But damn, if it wasn't *hard* not to.

But I did know she was thinking about me. I sensed it in History class. I saw how her body reacted to my closeness, how her pupils dilated and her breathing quickened when I leaned in towards her. Her body did not lie, despite what she might have said out loud. Abby pretended to be oblivious to how her body reacted to me, but I knew the truth. She knew the truth.

She wanted me.

And I wanted her.

I stepped away from the window and reached for my pen, clicking it repeatedly. I was nervous.

Giving her the textbook and writing that letter to her had been so thrilling I couldn't get it out of my mind all day. I ran through so many scenarios in my mind of her opening it up and reading it. How her pretty face would look when she read it. I honestly could not predict how she would react to my writing.

I had to wait and see.

And that was driving me mad.

Abby Starr was driving me mad.

This is unbearable.

I clicked my pen a dozen more times before throwing it in frustration back on my desk. I really couldn't deal with this waiting around. I simply wanted to know what she thought about that letter and about my truth I'd written down for her.

I can't predict what's going to happen when she does read it.

I thought Abby was a prude when I first met her outside my new house. I thought she was that goody-two-shoes neighbor. Your typical all-American girl next door. But, in the last few days, I'd come to realize there was a lot more going on in that house, and with Abby, than I first assumed. There was a darker side to her. A deeper side.

She was stronger than she let on.

And I wanted to know more.

Suddenly, there was movement across the yard. I rushed to the window to see the front door open and close.

It was Abby, and she was dressed in some garish colors. Brown and yellow.

What the fuck is she wearing?

A uniform.

Ah. I got it. She was going to work.

Perfect.

This was my chance.

As she started walking down the street, I pulled open my bedroom window and leaped outside. I landed on the soft grass and jumped the fence, running towards Abby.

Chasing her down the street.

I was out of breath by the time I'd caught up to her. She carried on walking, seemingly not surprised by my appearance. She knew I was there beside her, but didn't react. I walked shoulder-to-shoulder with her, staring at her until she turned to look at me.

"Hi," I said.

"Hey," she replied. She was completely emotionless. I guess that was for effect, to play hardball. To put me on edge.

It was working, I felt unease.

But I too could play that game.

"You off to work?" I asked.

"Yep."

"Did you open my present?"

"I did."

"Did you read the letter?"

"I did."

"And what do you think?" I asked, my voice rising.

Abby slightly smiled at me, her blue eyes glistening next. Unfazed. She flicked back her luscious dark brown hair and carried on walking down the street, completely ignoring my question.

Yeah, she's really putting me on edge.

"Are you going to reply or..."

Before I could finish my sentence, Abby thrust her fist towards me, pushing something into my hands.

I stopped to check what it was. A folded piece of paper, just like what I'd gifted to her earlier.

A letter.

I looked up to see that her pace hadn't stopped; she was already yards away from me, obviously not prepared to wait up. I got it. She wanted to give me that letter and get away from me. Make a big exit. How very dramatic.

I liked it.

"Thanks," I said in jest after her, but she didn't turn back.

* * *

"You should be careful about that Starr family."

I looked up from my plate. "What?" I asked.

I hadn't been listening to what my parents were talking about; I was too busy stuck in my own world, reliving the events of the school tour Abby gave me the day before. The way she fell into my hand placed on her cheek. The way her breath stopped as I pulled her into our secret place under the bleachers.

Those daydreams were so vivid in my mind that they were making me hard.

"The Starr family next door," Dad continued, irritated by my lack of attention. "You should be careful of them."

I stabbed at my peas with my fork. It was the start of yet another *family dinner* and Dad was already on one of his lectures.

"Why?" I asked, avoiding his eye contact.

"I saw one of them today. The mom, I believe."

"Right."

"She was staggering around outside their house looking like a drug addict, and you know what we think of them."

"The daughter is nice," I replied spitefully. It was pathetic, but I wasn't prepared to sit still and listen to Dad disparaging my neighbors.

"Her daughter? The one we met the other day?"

"Yeah. Her."

Dad chuckled to himself as if I'd muttered a joke. "She'll probably turn out like her mother, full of heroin or some other opioid."

I shook my head and went back to stabbing at my food. I was not going to be drawn into yet another argument with him. No way.

He could talk as much shit as he wanted about Abby and her family. It wouldn't change my mind about her at all.

"Drug addicts have it coming," Dad continued.

Here we go.

"Are you going to give us another one of your lectures, Dad?" I asked under my breath, but Dad was on a roll. Nothing I could say would stop him now.

"All I'm saying is that drug addicts wouldn't be in the position they're in if they had a little bit of *discipline*, that's all. They're punks. Lazy. They should just stop their intake of drugs and go and find a job. Make something of themselves. Stop bleeding taxpayers dry."

Great.

"I'm finished," I said, rising from the table and holding my plate.

Dad glared at me from across the table. "You'll sit until everyone else is finished," he barked.

"I'm eighteen, not a child anymore."

"You're in my house. My rules."

"I have homework to do."

He couldn't argue with that, but I did see his face redden with anger.

Good.

Just as I intended.

That's for insulting Abby, you bastard.

I ducked into the kitchen and washed my plate before

heading back into my bedroom, making sure my door was securely locked behind me. I wasn't going to let my parents disturb me, especially not now.

I reached under my bed and pulled out the bottle of vodka I had remaining from the other night and made myself comfortable at my desk. From my pocket, I took out the letter Abby had thrust into my hands earlier, opening it up for the first time. I'd saved reading it for this very moment, like it was a precious thing to be devoured only at a certain time.

Before I could fully unfold it, I could already tell it was short.

Very short.

I began to read the letter.

Dear Neighbor,

I suppose I should thank you for the textbook, and for your letter. So, here goes...

Thank you for the textbook and the letter.

THAT WAS IT?

That was all she had written to me?
That was her entire reaction to my letter?
It wasn't what I had planned.
I took a sip of the vodka and sighed.
Oh, Abby. You like to tease, don't you?

9

MILES

I was running late. Again.

Fuck.

As I dashed down the school hallways, I cursed the raging hangover burning in my head.

Why did I get so drunk the night before? What was I thinking?

I skidded to a stop in front of the classroom. Peeking through the door, I saw that History was already in session. Mrs. Winton stood in front of the class, gesticulating towards the whiteboard behind her which had a load of dates written down in columns.

Fuck.

I was very, very late.

Gingerly, I pressed open the door, trying not to make too much of a scene.

But that all went to shit the moment I stepped into the classroom.

"Late again are we, Mr. Hunter?" Mrs. Winton's face was a mixture of fury and exasperation as she spotted me ducking inside. I didn't blame her.

"Sorry," I grumbled, but it was not enough to placate her.

"This is the last time," the History teacher warned, poking a finger towards me. "The last time you're going to be late."

"Yes."

"I'm only letting you off the hook because you're new here, understood?"

The entire class was staring at us.

"Yes."

Well, thank fuck she hasn't realized how hungover I am.

She probably thought I was just lazy. Good.

I turned towards my desk, the eyes of the whole class staring back at me as I headed to my usual chair. I didn't really care about what any of them thought of me - I didn't even *know* any of their names - but there was one person who I did care about. One person whose eyes were shooting daggers in my directions.

Abby Starr.

She smirked at me triumphantly as I took my seat next to her. She was obviously enjoying my public humiliation very much.

Ugh.

I couldn't be dealing with her that day. I was in enough pain from the alcohol as it was.

She casually leaned over as I sat and whispered. "Hungover?"

I groaned in response and she moved away from me, satisfied to see me in such alcohol-fueled agony.

I'd gotten drunk the night before after I read her short,

blunt letter. I didn't know how to process her words, but I knew she was playing hard to get. She never even answered my probes about the kiss we shared, or how I wanted to see her again to "study" together. She was deliberately being coy and mysterious.

And it drove me insane.

That insanity drove me to drink the rest of that vodka bottle I had secretly saved. Much more than I intended.

And now, the next day in History class, I was paying the price of my late-night boozing.

As I watched Mrs. Winton drone on and on about Reconstruction or whatever, my heavy eyelids began to drop. I was so tired. I needed a nap. My hand balanced my head as I slipped away.

And, before I knew it, I was asleep.

I didn't know what I dreamed about, but it didn't feel like more than a second of darkness before I felt a sharp pain in my ribs.

"Ouch," I called out, blinking awake.

In front of me, the rest of the class was rushing out the door.

And next to me was Abby.

She elbowed me again in the ribs.

"Ouch, quit that."

"You're finally awake? Fantastic. Class is over," she said, her blue eyes trained on me.

"Right."

Abruptly, she stood up and left the classroom before I could talk to her properly. Before I could confront her about the letter she gave me the day before.

I had to speak to her.

It was the only reason I'd turned up to school that day in such a state. Why would I even go to school so hungover if it wasn't to speak to Abby Starr? I didn't give a shit about schoolwork.

Before the next class could arrive and take their seats, I pulled out a pen and piece of notepaper from my bag and quickly began to write.

DEAR NEIGHBOR,

Meet me in our spot next to the sports field after school.

I CHARGED out of the classroom, the note in my hand, and headed straight to the lockers. I'd bet she would be there.

And she was.

Alone.

No blonde-haired friend in sight.

Relief rushed through me as I bounded up to her. Abby was changing books in her locker, getting ready for her next class. She rolled her eyes when she saw me.

"Here," I said, offering out the folded note.

She looked down at the piece of paper dismissively and then up at me, not taking it. "What is it?" she asked.

"Read it."

"Nope."

My hand hovered between us, the note still outstretched towards her. She was going to take it, no matter what.

"How about you don't turn up drunk to school," she said, cold as ice.

I smiled at her. "I'm not drunk," I replied. "I'm *hungover*. Just take the damn thing off me, alright?"

Abby sighed, and in one quick move, snatched the piece of paper from my hand. She slammed the door to her locker shut and bounced away, giving me a generous look of her ass in her tight skirt.

She knew what she was doing. I saw the curve of her supple ass cheeks under the skirt as she walked away. The swaying of her hips. It was all on purpose. She wanted to get me hard.

She's really playing difficult, isn't she?

But I didn't care about her teasing. She had my note in her hand, and I just *knew* she was going to read it. I'd spiked her curiosity now.

She wouldn't be able to resist.

That was good enough for me.

* * *

I WAITED for her for a long time after school underneath the bleachers.

I watched the footballers head out for practice. I watched cheerleaders spy on them from the sidelines. I watched teachers head to their cars, bundles of notes weighing down their arms. I watched parents collect their children. I watched janitors empty the trash cans.

I watched for her.

But no Abby Starr.

She hadn't turned up.

She got my letter, but she clearly had decided not to come.

She thought she could ridicule me like this.

No. I wasn't going to give up that easily.

After an hour of waiting, I walked away from the bleachers. Yeah, I was a little bit embarrassed, but I was determined to talk to her. Properly this time.

I wanted a proper answer to my letter, and I was going to get it.

10

ABBY

I puffed through my lips.

"Do you really have to watch this movie?" I asked, facing my sister lying on the couch next to me.

"Yep," she replied, her focus fixated on the TV.

"Do you even like Frozen?"

"Yep."

"Aren't you a bit old for it?" I asked.

Serenity scrunched up her face at me as if I had said something completely stupid. "No."

I rolled my eyes and sank further into my seat. "Fine," I replied. "At least I have to go to work in a minute and not have to put up with this too long."

My sister gently kicked at me. I playfully slapped her foot away and turned back to the screen. Some snowman was singing. Any more of this insanity and I'd develop a migraine.

I checked the time on my phone, still too early to head into work.

But I could do with a leisurely walk.

I pulled myself up off the couch and reached for my bag.

"I'm going," I said to my sister. She smiled at me and continued watching the film. She'd taken her medicine, so I wasn't too worried about leaving her. I could have a stress-free shift.

My stepdad appeared in the hallway behind us. I sighed when I saw him. I really didn't want to deal with his shit.

"How about you hand over some of that money you make at work to your Mom," he said.

"Not this again."

"She gave birth to you. Show her some respect."

"Yeah," I replied. "And what else has she done since then? She doesn't pay for my sister's medication."

My stepdad had an awful body odor.

"But she is keeping you under her roof."

"Leave me alone, Cameron. I need to get to work."

Before I could react, his hand shot out and took tight hold of my wrist. His fingers burrowed into my skin. It was painful, but I didn't scream or cry out. I didn't want to give him the satisfaction that he was causing me pain. "You've got some bite to you," Cameron hissed quietly so that no one else could hear. Not my sister. Not my mom. "You better be careful with your teeth before they end you up in trouble one day."

I ripped my arm free from his grasp. "Piss off," I whispered sharply in reply.

I then quickly sprinted out of the house, flicking my head back over my shoulder to make sure my stepdad wasn't following. He wasn't.

I took in a few shallow breaths out on the sidewalk, trying to get my heart rate under control.

Just a few more weeks, Abby. A few more weeks until both you and Serenity are out of that house.

I couldn't wait.

I was so caught up with my future plans that I wasn't paying attention to where I was walking when I found myself nearly bumping into Miles.

"Whoah," I exclaimed as I stopped before we crashed into each other.

He stood in front of me on the street. Smiling.

He must've been coming from the other way. He must've seen me and deliberately ran into me.

"Hello, Abby."

"Hi, Miles."

He was wearing his familiar leather jacket and was looking as gorgeous as ever. His long blonde hair was wet and sleeked back. He'd probably just had a shower. He smelled fresh, too. Clean.

So incredibly good looking that it's exasperating.

He stood over me in his six-foot-something height. Dominating my space.

He must've been waiting for me. To ambush me there on the street as I passed his house.

"Did you read my note?" he asked.

"Yeah."

"Why didn't you come and meet me under the bleachers?"

I looked down and gestured at my gaudy uniform like it was obvious. "*Work.*"

Miles smiled again. "Right. So, you weren't standing me up?"

"Maybe that's what I'm trying to do now."

I brushed past him and continued walking towards the coffee shop. Yes, he was drop-dead gorgeous, but that didn't mean I had an obligation to give him the time of day.

Miles rushed up to walk beside me. I avoided his stare, looking straight ahead.

"So, how about it?" he asked.

I flicked my hair back. "How about what?"

"You and me. Catching up on History together."

"Well, what do you want to know?"

"Everything."

I smirked at him. "Let me see. There was a Big Bang, then there were dinosaurs, then Jesus, then the War of Independence, and then there was us."

Miles chuckled. "Not like that."

"Really? What would you like then?"

"I would like us two to sit down together and talk."

I raised an eyebrow. "Talk about what?"

Miles shrugged. "History."

"History of the world?" I asked. "Or our personal history?"

Miles twisted in close towards me. I could smell his sweet aftershave and feel his warm breath on my neck. "Anything you desire," he muttered, and I felt the space between my legs heat up. "Anytime you want."

I stopped. We'd made it to outside my work. The franchise coffee shop. "How about now?" I asked, gesturing to the front glass doors. Miles blinked, realizing what I meant.

"In there?"

"That's where I work."

He took it all in.

"Sure."

I pulled out my phone, checking the time. I flashed a smile at my neighbor. "I have half an hour before my shift starts."

He shrugged.

"Let's do it."

* * *

"You want a coffee?" I asked, as Miles opened his textbook at the table.

He looked up at me, his bright blue eyes piercing. "Sure," he said.

I couldn't avoid staring at his thin scar. The way it slightly tilted when he spoke. The way it followed the sharp line of his jaw. He said he got it in a fight. It must've been a vicious one to damage him so.

I wonder what he did to the other guy.

Miles did say he was defending a girl from some dude who was insulting her.

Yeah, what a knight in shining armor. Not.

"Give me two secs," I replied, dropping my bag on my seat and heading behind the counter.

My friend Charlotte had already started her shift. She also worked at the coffee place with me. As Miles and I entered the coffee shop, I spied her delightfully surveying us, and when I ducked behind the counter to get us the coffees, she was still keeping a rabid eye on me.

"What?" I asked her, bashful. I knew my cheeks must've been flushed red.

"Nothing."

"Don't you dare say anything," I warned jokingly.

She raised her arms up. "Hey, I'm not saying anything."

I giggled. "Sure."

I made Miles and I two lattes on the espresso machine, bringing them back to the table. Miles was waiting for me to come back, his textbook and notepad open and ready. He took the offered cup with a grin.

"Thanks," he said.

"Probably a little better than vodka," I replied.

"Don't you dare start."

"Right. Let's get down to it."

We spent the next fifteen minutes going through the basics of what we'd been through in History class. It turned out that Miles had been studying most of the same stuff in his old school, so there wasn't too much detail I needed to fill him up on.

But we weren't really there for schoolwork.

I knew that. He knew that.

This is all just a game we're playing between us.

I couldn't shake off the tension of being so close to him. I tried to act normal, act like my heart wasn't racing and my breathing wasn't fast, but it was hard to hide my thirst.

Miles was somehow calm and relaxed.

Damn him.

He didn't try anything. He didn't need to. Being in such tight proximity was enough for both of us. He listened hard to what I said, asking all the right questions. He made the study easy. I found myself weirdly comfortable around him, despite the stormy electricity between us.

And, sometimes, I found myself staring at his scar and wanting desperately to kiss it. Bite it. Taste it.

Time flew by, and suddenly I had to start my shift.

"This was fun," Miles said as we closed his textbook and I stood up from the table. "We need to do this again sometime."

"Maybe."

"Maybe?"

I winked. "We'll see."

"You're gonna leave me hanging like that?" he asked.

"Yep," I replied, bouncing away from him to around the coffee shop counter. Miles didn't attempt to say anything else to me. He left the coffee shop biting his lower lip, happy.

Oh, how I wished I could feel that lip on mine again.

"So, what's this?" Charlotte asked, skipping over to me beside the tills.

"It's nothing," I said.

"Yeah. *Sure.* I see what's going on."

"It really is nothing," I replied. "He needed help catching up on History. He wanted my help."

"Surely that wasn't the only thing he needed help with."

"Shut up, Charlotte."

"Maybe it wasn't just History he needed help with, maybe you should've gone over Chemistry."

I blinked. "Chemistry? Why?"

"Because I was seeing a whole load of chemistry between you two."

I suppressed a laugh at my friend's awful pun. "Okay, now you need to *really* shut up."

"I'm not saying anything."

"Okay."

She leaned in close to me. "He is pretty hot, though."

I didn't reply. Instead, I turned to the next customer to serve.

But Charlotte was right.

Miles was pretty hot. Was I falling for him?

11

MILES

"You're actually on time for once," Abby smarmily greeted me as I sat down at the desk next to her in the History classroom. I slid into my usual leaning posture and raised my eyebrows at her.

"And you're actually already at your desk," I shot back. "You're early. What a little suck up you are."

Abby poked her tongue out at me in response and I smirked back.

She leaned over to sort through her bag, giving me a perfect view of her ass under her skirt. I caught a glimpse of her panties, and I felt the heat rush to my cock. Making me hard.

Fuck.

I didn't plan on getting a boner in class that day.

Abby straightened up, limiting my sight of her tight little ass, and pulled out her History textbook from her bag. The textbook *I'd* given her.

She knew what she was doing.

I would do anything to rip her skirt off right here and now.

"How's the book going?" I asked. "Learned anything yet?"

"More than you," she replied. "You still need coaching?"

I shrugged my shoulders. "Well, I do have the hots for my private tutor. I wouldn't say no to another lesson."

Abby rolled her eyes at my lewd comment and turned away from me. I liked how much I infuriated her. I bet I annoyed her so much that I was the only thing playing in her mind. If there was one thing I knew about girls, it was that if you could make them laugh, scream, or cry, then they would never forget you. Sometimes they would go *crazy* over you just because you irritated the hell out of them.

And I hoped Abby was going crazy for me.

Because, *hell*, I was going crazy for her.

Mrs. Winton walked into the room and started the class. She began writing on the whiteboard, talking about something to do with Lincoln, but I was already zoning out.

I was daydreaming about Abby. Thinking about us fucking. Thinking about grabbing her silky white ass and pinching it between my fingers. Spanking her. Making her moan.

I was brought back to reality by a poke in my arm. It was Abby, her arm outstretched as Mrs. Winton droned on at the front of the class. In my neighbor's hand was a piece of paper.

Her eyes darted down at it, inviting me to take the paper.

Stealthily, I seized it off her and opened it between the pages of my textbook to avoid Mrs. Winton's attention.

DEAR NEIGHBOR,

You want another lesson with your hot private History tutor?

Meet me on my way to work this afternoon.

Same time as yesterday.

SMILING, I flipped over the note to the blank side and scribbled in my response.

*Y*ES.

I FLICKED it over to Abby. She caught it quietly and quickly scanned my reply.

She didn't say a word. She didn't react. She just tore the piece of paper up in front of her to hide the evidence.

It was the sexiest thing I'd seen her do.

The class went by. Abby and I didn't get the chance to talk anymore. Mrs. Winton spoke for the rest of the lesson and, when the bells rang at the end of class, Abby's blonde friend rushed over to her to whisper in her ear something I couldn't decipher. They scampered out of the classroom together, giggling, with the rest of the students, leaving me alone.

I shook my head and leaned over to collect my bag.

Abby knew how to keep me guessing, that was for sure. She knew how to tease me.

I wandered the school hallways, not bothering to show up for my next lesson. The school, despite Abby's tour the other day, was still completely foreign to me, and I didn't feel the need to bother learning its layout only a few weeks from finishing.

I passed the sports trophy cabinet with all the gold and bronze medals inside, then onto the school noticeboard. It was littered with posters for Prom. I'd absolutely forgotten about it.

It was next week.

Next Friday.

* * *

I SAT on the edge of my bed and contemplated whether to open a new bottle of vodka. I was practically reaching for it.

But a small voice spoke to me from the back of my head. Telling me no.

That small voice sounded a lot like Abby's.

I sighed and stood up, walking towards my window. I checked the time on my phone. That same time yesterday was when Abby left for work, so I should be seeing her any minute skip out of her front door. I peered through my bedroom window towards her house and waited.

Any minute now.

I could take a sip from the bottle. Loosen up a little.

No.

I shouldn't do that. Plus, Abby would be able to smell it on me. She seemed not to like it when I drank.

I leaned against the window.

And then, like clockwork, the front door of the house opposite my room swung open, and out stepped Abby. My heart caught in my throat when I saw her. Every time I saw her, my body froze. She had a weird spell over me, something I hadn't felt for any other girl. She touched me in ways inside that I'd never experienced before.

I didn't move, I just observed her bouncing to the front of her yard, flipping her head towards my house. No doubt looking for me. Waiting for me.

Goddamn, that was cute. I liked the way she searched for me.

So, she wasn't completely heartless after all. She wasn't completely cold to me.

I knew she held some deeper feelings for me than she let on.

Time to put her out of her misery. I checked my bedroom door was locked, silently opened my window, and rolled outside. Mindful of my parents discovering my escape. I leaped across the yard right up to Abby, scaring her.

She jumped when she saw me, not expecting me to

come bounding up to her like that. Her gasp made me laugh.

"Here I am," I announced, my arms wide. She playfully shoved me away.

"Don't scare me like that."

"Why not? It was fun."

"Not for me."

I laughed again, and she shot me a frown. "You like it, come on."

"You're so..."

"Gorgeous? Handsome? Sexy? Charming?"

Abby placed her hands on her hips. "*Infuriating*," she replied.

"So, you've decided to give me another go? Even if I'm super infuriating?"

"Only another go at tutoring. You need to catch up." Abby started to walk. "Don't you get any ideas that this is more than that."

"Hey, you're the one who's said that there's more than just tutoring going on here. I never, for one moment, even *thought* this meant anything more."

She huffed at me. "Okay."

"I mean, if you want to *call* this a *date* or whatever, that's completely up to you."

Abby laughed and shook her head. "Be careful. You're crossing the line, mister."

"Fine, then," I replied. "This is definitely not a date. Got that."

"Yep."

"Just two friends going to get coffee together."

"*And studying*," Abby added quickly.

"Sure, and that too."

"Good. I'm glad you understand."

"You're the one who raised the topic."

"Whatever."

I kept up with her as we rounded our block towards her coffee shop.

"Did you know Prom was next week?" I asked. I don't know why I asked her that, but the posters I saw back at school had somehow imprinted themselves into my mind all afternoon. I hadn't even thought about Prom until I saw them.

If I was going, then I wanted to take her with me.

"Yeah, I did," Abby replied. "My friend, Charlotte, can't shut up about it. She's trying to get one of the footballers to ask her out."

"How's it going for her?"

"She's giving off all the right signs. She's been flirting with him between every class and being all girlish around him. It's pretty obvious what she wants him to do, but I think he's a bit clueless about it all. It's up to him now to bite the bullet and actually ask her."

"Right," I said, kicking a pebble that had gotten loose from the sidewalk. "Are you going?"

"Yeah."

That's your cue.

My hands shook, so I dug them deep into my leather jacket. I don't know why I was so nervous. I was never like this.

Just ask her, dude.

"You're going with anyone?"

Abby snorted. It was cute, but it also drove me mad. Was she laughing at me? "Why are you asking?"

"I dunno," I replied.

There was a pause that seemed to stretch for eternity between us. We carried on walking but were completely silent until Abby spoke again.

"Is this a long-winded way of you asking me out?"

This was my time to snort. "Nope. Proms are stupid."

"Right, you're so *cool* and *above* the rest of us, right?" she asked.

"No. I just don't like dressing up and being all forced into a weird social interaction like that."

"Such a rebel. I mean, *dressing up?* All I ever see you in is that leather jacket."

I laughed. "You don't like it?"

"I never said that."

"So, you think it fits well on me?"

Abby rolled her eyes. "I never said that either."

"You like me in it, don't you deny it."

"You're crossing the line again there, Miles."

"So, no boyfriend to take you to Prom?"

"Why are you so insistent on knowing about my love life, Miles?"

"We're study partners. We should get to know each other."

I waited for Abby's answer, but she didn't talk. We continued walking. I could see her work ahead of us. We were close.

"If you must know," Abby said quietly as we nearly reached the front doors of her coffee shop. "I've never had a boyfriend."

What?

"None?"

"None," she replied.

That probably makes her a virgin, doesn't it?

I didn't expect her to say that. I was sure a girl that pretty would have guys falling at her feet.

"I mean, that's cool."

"Is it though? Sounds pretty geeky to me."

The last thing I was going to do was shame her or anything. I didn't even think there was any shame in being a virgin, but I could see from her shy eyes that she was divulging something that made her feel incredibly self-conscious. This wasn't the self-assured sassy Abby I knew. She was revealing something vulnerable to me now. And it was my job to listen, and not judge.

"No, it isn't."

Abby wiped her eyes with the back of her sleeve. I noticed a single tear welling up. "It's just been... *difficult* with my sister and everything. I've just never had the time for a guy."

Her sister?

I didn't know anything about her sister. I didn't even know she had one. This was something I would have to find out more about.

Whatever she was telling me was straight from the heart. It was almost like a privilege hearing Abby confess to me like this.

"Your sister?" I asked.

"She has some... medical issues. It feels weird saying this."

Oh, I see.

"You don't have anything to feel weird about," I reassured her as she dabbed away the tears on her cheeks. "Hey, and you're not a geek. Trust me. I don't think I've met a geek as hot as you before."

She dried her eyes and the old sassy Abby returned. She grinned at me, her pale face angelically shining in the afternoon sunlight.

"And what about you, Miles?"

"Me?"

"Any *chicks* in your life?" she asked.

I reached over her shoulder for the door to her coffee shop. Very close to her. "I've been around the block, but there's this *sexy* private tutor who's teaching me History I'll like to screw around with."

Abby laughed and skipped inside. "Shut up," she replied, kicking at me.

Yep, the sassy old Abby was back.

And I still hadn't asked her out to Prom.

12

ABBY

I WATCHED Miles leave the coffee shop. He turned back to me and winked. Startled by his overpowering and sudden attention, I looked down, blushing. By the time I faced up again, he was gone, out of the glass door and onto the street.

He had transfixed me.

"Yeah, you definitely have the hots for him," Charlotte whispered in my ear as she passed behind me, giving me a playful jab in the side with her fingers. I wriggled away from her and shot her a dirty look.

"Shut up," I replied. "I don't."

"You so do."

"Nope."

"Yep. I've been spying on both of you every day for the past four days. You both have been pretty consistent. Anyone with half a brain could see the way you *stare* at him."

"I don't stare."

"It doesn't take a lot to know what's happening between you two."

"Which is?"

Charlotte backed away towards the tills with a cheeky smile on her face. "You know what it is, Abby. Don't play dumb."

I rolled my eyes at my friend and turned to the espresso machine, waiting for the next order to make.

Miles and I had been meeting up routinely for the past few days, him rushing out of his window to greet me before I headed into work. We would walk together, flirting and gently ribbing each other, before we took our seats at the coffee shop where we would study for half an hour before I had to start work.

And every day Charlotte had been watching us from behind the coffee shop counter.

She was right, though. The chemistry between Miles and I was pretty obvious. We were good together. He made me snort with laughter and I was a good tutor for him. We were a good team.

We had been getting super close, and that fact had slowly dawned on me until I could no longer pretend to deny it and it was staring at me in the face. It was too late to do anything about our intimacy, but I think I was slowly *falling* for the guy.

Ugh.

Why now?

"Two lattes and a cappuccino, takeaway," Charlotte called to me from the tills, breaking me out of my daydreams. I began making the coffees, thinking of Miles's full lips and the delicate scar that hung over them.

I finished the coffees and handed them over to the customer.

"So," Charlotte gossiped quietly. "Is this going to be a *thing* now?"

"What is?"

"Really, Abby. As I said, don't play dumb. It doesn't suit you," she replied. She had me all figured out. "Are you and Miles going to be a thing?"

"I dunno."

"Has he asked you out to Prom yet?"

He hasn't. And he had the chance.

"Charlotte." I slapped her on the shoulder. My friend giggled. She had me on the ropes.

"So that's a *no*, then? But I bet you want him to."

"He thinks Proms are stupid."

"Every boy says that."

"I think he means it."

"So what if he thinks they're stupid? He should take you there, anyway."

I sighed. "He's... *we're* not really like that. It seems, whatever we have, to be pretty private."

"Sounds like you're making excuses for him to act like an asshole."

"Ugh, Charlotte. You're so annoying."

A customer appeared in front of the counter, ready to order. I skipped back over to the coffee machine, grateful to be out of Charlotte's inquisitive firing line for a moment.

I knew I had my first impression of Miles completely wrong. Sure, he liked to think and act like a bad boy, but I knew he wasn't really like that. The way he acted with me proved that. I had him wrong when I first tried to shake his hand, and I knew he felt the same way.

His reaction the other day when I practically revealed I was a virgin cemented him in my eyes. I didn't even know why I said it, it just came out of me, but Miles was so supportive of me. I could tell he cared for me. It'd been a long time since any boy ever showed me that side to them. If ever.

I made the new coffee order, smiling to myself.

Maybe I did have the hots for him. Maybe it was too late for me.

13

ABBY

THE CAFETERIA WAS ALREADY HEAVING with students by the time Charlotte and I took our usual seats.

I placed my tray on the table and popped open my can of Diet Coke with a hiss.

I took a sip of the ice-cold drink and flipped my attention onto Charlotte. "So, has Martin finally stepped up and asked you to Prom yet?"

My friend puffed and slowly shook her head at my question. "I'm still working on him."

"I see."

"He'll ask me out. Eventually."

"Eventually."

"I just have to pull it out of his stupid skull."

"Right."

"Hey, you can't talk. What's happening with your neighbor?"

I gave her a death stare. "Don't start on that. Not again."

It had only been the night before when Charlotte had

asked me about Miles taking me to Prom. I thought I had dispelled her inquisitiveness. But nope. She was still keen to press me on him.

"All I see is you two together," my friend said, smirking.

"Okay, you're going there?"

"I am," she replied. "It's fun that you're having a bit of drama. For once."

"You're enjoying it?"

"Sure am."

"Well, I'm not."

I took another sip of Diet Coke and stared down at my food. I wasn't hungry.

"There he is." Charlotte pointed her burger across the cafeteria. To an empty table on the other side of the room. A table empty except for one person.

Miles.

He sat alone with a tray of food in front of him, his head bowed. He didn't seem fussed about being the only one in the room without any friends. He didn't seem uncomfortable at all that he was on his own. Rare for a high school student.

We watched on as someone approached his table. Marsha. The head cheerleader and the high school's most popular girl. She ate boys for breakfast and crushed "average" girls like Charlotte and me under her foot for fun.

She was the highest on the food chain around there. The rest of us were just living in her world.

She was approaching Miles with her famous sexy strut. The one that reliably got all males within eyeshot to gawk and stare every time she passed. She liked to deploy that strut whenever she graced the hallways of the school, and it always worked to great effect.

My focus shifted from Marsha to her usual table. The

rest of the cheerleading squad sat, rapt, as their leader strutted her stuff over to the mysterious loner boy.

This isn't going to end well.

"Poor Miles," Charlotte remarked, also staring on. I agreed with her. He was a goner.

I looked around. It seemed like the entire cafeteria had their eyes on Marsha and Miles, waiting to see what was going to happen. Waiting for blood. By heading over to the new boy, the head cheerleader was making a peacock display of her popularity. Asserting her dominance. Her being interested in him meant that he was now her property to do with what she pleased. And we'd all seen this exact scenario play out a hundred times before.

Yep. Poor Miles.

He still had his head down over his food, completely oblivious to the new attention placed on him. Marsha strutted right up to him.

Her mouth started moving. Talking. Straining, I still couldn't overhear what she was saying, but I didn't even need to. Everyone in that cafeteria knew what she was doing. She was seducing him, either to laugh at him or for a short public fling. She did this with the most desired boys. All the football team had gone out with her at some point, mainly for the popularity of being with the most desired girl in the school. Something about Miles - his mysteriousness, perhaps, or his good looks - had made him a glowing red target for her. He couldn't escape now. She had him in her talons.

And why do I feel a pang of jealousy?

Marsha finished speaking, her lips pouting towards Miles.

My new neighbor didn't seem to move at all. His head was still bowed. He still seemed wrapped up in his own world.

But then he looked up. He locked eyes with Marsha. A short sentence came out of his gorgeous mouth. That was it.

And then I saw the strangest sight. Marsha stamped her foot and let out a gasp. A tantrum. I'd never seen her react that way. Certainly not in public like this.

Miles had clearly given her an answer she didn't see coming.

And then she was storming away from him, red-faced. Upset. Angry.

Yeah, that had never happened before.

"Her knickers are in a twist," Charlotte remarked, as dumbfounded as I was.

Miles resumed leaning over his food, his face obscured by his long, blonde hair.

What had just happened?

Marsha disappeared into a huddle of the cheerleaders, and the rest of the cafeteria went back to their food, whispering excitedly over what had just occurred. Guessing. I could hear what they were talking about. Who was that strange boy? Is he weird or something?

Miles was back to sitting at that table alone. The other students or their opinions didn't faze him at all.

Charlotte and I looked at each other in disbelief.

Miles had done something no other guy had done.

He'd *rejected* Marsha.

"He's all on his own now," Charlotte pointed out. "Maybe you should keep him company."

She meant it mockingly, but I took it as a challenge.

"Yeah, why not?" I stood from the table, leaving behind the food I had no appetite for, and began to march across the cafeteria towards Miles.

"Hey, Abby," Charlotte called after me. I gave her a quick smile and continued walking.

Serves her right for being so smarmy.

I breathed a sigh of relief. Marsha had already left the room with her gaggle of cheerleaders. I couldn't deal with her getting angry over what I was about to do.

I reached Miles' table. His head was still bowed, eating. He paid no attention to the rest of the room. He didn't even notice me until I leaped up onto the table so that I sat facing him, only inches apart.

I only hoped I got a better treatment from him than Marsha did.

"Hi, Miles," I cooed.

He nonchalantly turned his head to look up at me. When he noticed it was me, he flashed me a lazy grin.

"Hi, Abby."

I watched his eyes scour over me, taking my body in. My short skirt. My perky breasts under my top. The way I sat, with my ass on top of the table, gave him a perfect view of my full body. I saw the desire in his eyes like a little fire that grew into a raging blaze.

I liked how much I turned him on.

"What you doing?" I asked.

Miles nodded towards his tray of food. "Eating."

I leaned over. He had nothing but a load of fries on his tray. No signs of anything else.

"Just fries?"

"Why not?"

"Seems a little... odd," I replied.

Miles shrugged. "They're my favorite food."

I giggled. "Still strange."

"Why not eat your favorite food, Abby? Why not treat yourself? Life is short."

"Is that a line you use on all the girls?"

He winked. "Sometimes."

"I saw you and Marsha together."

He rolled his eyes. "Oh, so that's her name?"

"It seems like you upset her."

"Seems like I did."

"What did you say?"

He smiled at me again. A slight smile full of gratification. He was pleased with himself. "I told her where to go."

"Right."

Damn, he really likes being mysterious, doesn't he?

I patted down my skirt and stared at him. His blue eyes stared back at me. Penetrating me. Deeply. There was definitely something between us. Something I couldn't shake off, no matter how hard I tried. "How are you feeling about the new school?" I asked.

"There are one or two attractive students."

"You mean, Marsha?"

His face turned serious. "No. There's only one student I find attractive."

I laughed nervously. He could be so disarming. "But, seriously, though. How are you finding the place?"

Miles reached forward to pick up another fry. He took a bite. "It's better than my last place."

"The place where you got into a fight?"

"Yep."

"What happened there?"

Miles ate another golden fry. "I got into a fight. I got bashed up. The other guy had it worse. That's it."

"And you moved schools because of it?"

"Yep. Moved schools and moved towns. It was either that or the Army."

I did a double-take. "The Army?"

Miles chuckled. "Dad was in the Army. I grew up in a military household. I've been warned in no uncertain terms that if I get into another fight, that's it for me. *Zip.* Straight off to the Army." He flicked at a fry to emphasize his point.

"But you're eighteen," I exclaimed. "You can make your own decisions whether or not to join the military."

"You don't know my dad. He's got ways of forcing me into shit. And, besides, maybe the Army *is* the best place for me. I don't really have any other skills other than to stand up straight and take orders."

I thought back on that clean-cut man I met that day Miles's family moved in next door. That perfect-posture man with the buzz cut who tightly shook my hand. Miles' dad.

He must be one hell of a bastard to make Miles feel this way.

"And what about you?" Miles asked, leaning back into his seat and casually scooping a handful of fries into his mouth. "What are you going to do with yourself once you graduate?"

"That's easy."

His eyebrows raised. "Oh, you have it all figured out?"

"Yep."

"So?"

"So. I'm out of here. Moving away."

"Where to?"

"I dunno. Anywhere but here, though," I replied. "And I'm taking my sister with me."

"Your sister?"

I'd barely mentioned my sister in my lessons with Miles. I barely mentioned her with anyone, even Charlotte. I wanted to keep my normal life separate from what happened at home. I wanted to keep my friends away from my stepdad and my Mom. I was so embarrassed by what went on inside my house and didn't want anyone else to share in it.

"Serenity. I'm going to adopt her and we're gonna leave here."

"Why so?" Miles asked.

I sighed. "My family. Mom and my stepdad are not... my favorite people. I need to get out."

"Oh, okay."

I had tried to explain my sister to Miles the other day, but I couldn't get the right words out.

Here I'll try again.

"Serenity has had medical issues her whole life. I want to drag her away from here, give her a good home with me. Just get away from my stepdad."

"It's that bad?"

I nodded, forcing back the tears. I didn't mean to cry, not in my school's cafeteria and especially not in front of Miles. But there I was, blubbering again.

I held the waterworks back, though.

"Well, you seem to have it all figured out. Unlike me."

I nodded weakly. "I do."

"Here," Miles said, offering a single fry towards me. "Have one of these. I guarantee it'll make you feel better."

I laughed and took the food off him, placing it in my mouth. Hot and salty. "Thanks."

"See? Much better."

I smiled. "Yep. Much better."

Miles flicked a fry at me. It flew into my face. He laughed, and I giggled.

Yep, a much better treatment than Marsha got.

14

ABBY

INSIDE THE KITCHEN, I finished draining the pasta over the sink and picked up the jar of pesto. I stirred the green mixture into the pan and licked my fingers. It smelled delicious. I poured the pasta into two bowls and headed down the hallway.

I knocked on my sister's room. Hearing Serenity call out for me to enter, I opened the door with my spare elbow and sashayed into the bedroom.

"Bon appetite," I announced, raising up the two bowls of steaming pesto pasta in my hands. My sister sat up in her chair, excited to finally eat.

"Thanks," she said as I placed one bowl in front of her.

"Make sure you take your pills before you eat," I reminded her, casting a glance towards the medication on her shelf. Serenity sighed and reached for the pills, popping them on her tongue before she put a huge forkful of pasta into her mouth.

"How is it?" I asked.

"Yeah, good."

We ate in silence for a while, the only sound coming from our forks scratching against the bowls.

Serenity finished her pasta first. "You know that new neighbor?" she asked, placing her empty bowl on her desk beside her.

"What? Miles?"

"Yeah, him."

I scooped up a chunk of pasta onto my fork. "Not this again."

"I saw him with you yesterday," Serenity said.

I opened my mouth, nearly spitting out pesto. "What?"

Shit, shit, shit.

"Yeah, you two were walking down the street. I saw you from my window. You were talking together."

"You did?"

My sister eyed me suspiciously. "Yeah. I did. What are you doing with him?"

I pulled my focus back down to my bowl, playing with my pasta. "I tutor him," I replied, trying hard to appear nonchalant. "My teacher asked me to help him catch up on History. Plus, he lives next door, so it was easy enough to meet up like that. We're friendly."

"Well, you two looked pretty close to me."

I growled. "We're not."

"You looked more than just *friendly*."

"Nope."

"Right."

My sister could see through my bullshit.

"Why do you care, anyway?" I asked.

Serenity absentmindedly spun around in her chair. "I don't, really. It's just that I also saw him the other night."

"You did?"

"He was drinking."

"Where?"

"Just in the yard between our houses."

"Yeah? The bastard."

"He looked kinda sad."

I chortled. "He's *cocky*, but he isn't sad."

My sister shrugged. "That's what I saw. That's all I'm saying."

"You don't know him."

"Okay," my sister replied, crossing her arms. "You tell me about him then, seeing as you both are so *friendly*."

"Yeah, we're friends. Nothing more." I placed my bowl next to hers. "He told me about his family. His dad was in the military. He might be forced into it himself."

"Does he even want to?"

"I dunno.," I replied.

"Do you want him to?"

"Huh?"

"Would you like him to join up with the Army?"

"Why would I care?"

Serenity huffed like I was purposely acting stupid. "He's basically your boyfriend."

"It doesn't work like that, Serenity," I replied. "I don't even know what's going on between us."

"So, there is *something* going on."

"I didn't say that," I barked back. "It's just he's very *flirty* and I'm..."

"You."

I chuckled. "Precisely. I'm not giving much back."

"Yeah."

I reached out and held her leg warmly. "There's a lot for me to think about before I even dare think about *boys*. You're more special to me than some boy who lives next door, no matter even if he has nice eyes and a sexy leather jacket."

My sister giggled and grabbed the two plates.

"Let's wash these up and watch a movie," she suggested.

"Good idea."

* * *

I LAY IN BED, unable to sleep, when I heard a knock on my window.

A gentle tapping.

I didn't have to get up to know who it was.

Miles.

I refused to leave the house, so instead, I climbed over to the window and opened it up. Miles stood there, head reaching the windowsill, his leather jacket on and his gorgeous smile across his face.

"Where were you this afternoon?" he asked me, blue eyes glinting at me like two bright lights in the night.

I ignored his dumb question.

"What are you doing here?" I hissed at him, mindful of waking up my house. "It's the middle of the night. You shouldn't be doing this."

"I had a feeling you'd be awake," my neighbor whispered quickly back. "Answer my question. I asked you, where were you this afternoon?"

"What do you mean?"

"I didn't see you head off to work."

"It was my day off."

"And you didn't tell me?"

"You know," I replied. "I actually *don't* have to tell you everything going on in my life."

"What about History?"

"You couldn't go one day without studying it?"

Miles leaned forward so that his face was inside my bedroom. "I couldn't go one day without seeing you."

"Shut up," I replied.

But then he kissed me.

His lips touched mine and, before I knew it, he had his hands running through my hair. I was shocked, then confused, and then I melted into his kiss. It felt like my soul left my body and was floating above me, looking down at Miles wrapping himself around me. He was strong and overpowering. And I loved it.

The kiss was even better than the first time he kissed me, practically in the same spot next to my window. This time he didn't reek of alcohol. This time he was in charge, getting what he wanted. And I let him.

And then it was over. I didn't want it to end, but he was off me.

It all happened so quickly. One moment he was there, his head in my window, kissing me, and then he let go of me. He was outside. Then he shot me a flash of a smile.

And then he was gone.

Disappeared.

Like the ghost he was.

Back to his house.

I watched the back of him as he leaped over the fence separating our two bedrooms. He had run away as quickly as he appeared at my window. A blur of a man. My neighbor who came over because he was horny and got what he wanted. A kiss.

And then he left. Almost as if he wanted to confuse me more.

I had done something similar to him. This time, he was getting his revenge.

But it still hit me hard in the heart.

I slumped back inside my bedroom, quietly shutting my window. I wandered over to my bed and slipped back in, still so bewildered by the speed of what had just happened.

One moment our lips were touching, then the next he was gone.

Did he know how much he was teasing me?

Did he know how fast he made my heart beat?

Did he know how much he made my head spin?

I pulled the bedcovers over me and closed my eyes.

I didn't know what to think of Miles. Was he just playing with me? Was it fun to mess around with me, knowing that I was a virgin and inexperienced with boys? Was that all I was to him? A new toy that made things easier by living next door? He was so sure and confident in himself, I had to doubt his intentions.

And what did I want with him? Straight after graduation in a few weeks, I was going to be out of that house, no matter what. Where would that leave us?

Everything that had happened between us, and what *could* happen, was so up in the air because our futures were uncertain. School was ending soon. We would have to be adults. Forced to go out in the big, bad world. We would have to choose our own paths in life. We would naturally split apart.

The kiss was nice and welcome. But what did it mean? And did it even mean anything at all?

Did I even want to kiss him back? I did at that moment, but I was wary of getting my heart involved. Not now. I didn't want it to break.

I fell asleep not knowing what to do, or where I stood with that guy next door.

15

MILES

THE DAY AFTER THE KISS, I didn't see Abby. It was like she had disappeared. I didn't see her when I wandered around the school hallways. I didn't see her out in the sports field. I didn't have History, so I didn't see her then. I looked around for her everywhere in that stupid old brick building. She was practically the only reason why I still went to school, but I couldn't find that beautiful girl anywhere.

She could've been hiding from me.

There was no way she didn't like the kiss the night before. She *leaned* into me as I leaned into her bedroom window. I felt then how eager she was to kiss me back.

But, as I walked around the hallways of the school, I was still worried I had done something wrong.

I had never been so strung up about a girl before. Usually, I would just fuck them and break up. Leaving them in shreds of tears. But not Abby. We hadn't even screwed around yet, something I would usually get over with after the first date. And had we even been on dates?

Our coffee shop lessons weren't exactly *romantic*, but I enjoyed them much more than anything else in my life. I would wait for them all day. Wait for the moment I would see Abby unlock her front door in her ugly work uniform.

Yeah, I'm really getting caught up with this girl.

And the funny thing was that I didn't care. I actually *wanted* to see her. I *wasn't* planning on running away from her.

What have I become?

It was late in the afternoon after I'd come home from school and had dinner when I heard the knocking on my bedroom door.

I sat up in bed when I heard the tapping.

"Come in."

It was Dad. He marched into the room in his usual sharp militaristic style, narrowed eyes searching the place from top to bottom as he stomped inside.

"Can I help you?" I asked him. Despite my rebellious nature, I still jumped out of bed and practically stood at attention when he entered. When I was a kid, Dad used to command me around like that, as if we were practicing Army drills. Even when I was eighteen, it was instinctive to do it. Old habits die hard, I guess.

Dad ignored my question and started exploring around the room, checking behind my desk, my shelves, and my floor. He was looking for something, but I didn't know what. I watched him as his clean-cut clenched jaw scoped around my bedroom, intensely searching.

"What are you looking for?" I asked him.

Dad turned to me then, marching straight up to my face so that we were inches apart. I could smell his minty breath. His dark eyes scanned me up and down and I could make out the pulsing vein on his forehead. He was agitated, that was for sure.

"Alcohol," he seethed. His mouth transformed into a snarl and his face went red. "I know you have some in here."

"I don't know what you're talking about."

"Don't take me for an idiot, boy."

"I'm not."

"I know you drink. I know you keep a stash of alcohol hidden in here somewhere."

"I don't."

"Don't play silly games with me. I know you, son."

"I don't doubt it."

That made him really mad. Dad pointed a wavering finger at me. "You drink, I know you do. It's my fault. I should've been stricter on you when you were younger. I let you get away with too much. I should've beaten that naughty streak out of you when I had the chance."

"You could still beat me if you'd like," I replied, smirking.

Try it, big guy.

I couldn't help myself. I just had to wind him up. He was in my room and intimidating me. It was the least I could do.

Dad's face turned an even brighter shade of red and his eyes went wild.

"You want a fight, boy?" A piece of his spit flew out from between his front teeth and landed on my shoulder. He either didn't notice the droplet or he didn't care.

I crossed my arms and went silent. There was no reasoning with my father, especially when he was in a state like this. A state he seemed to permanently be in these days.

I mean, he *was* right. I did drink. I did hide bottles of alcohol in my room. I just thought I kept it hidden from him. That's why I usually drank at night, with my door locked. I mostly snuck outside and drank in the yard between mine and Abby's house, away from him and his prying eyes.

I knew I'd soon be an alcoholic at the rate I was going.

And, before I met Abby, I didn't care. I didn't care where my life was heading, even though I knew exactly what I was doing.

But then I met her, and everything changed. I had a reason to wake up in the morning. To see her in History class. To sit next to her. To smell her sweet perfume. To taste her soft lips.

I finally had something - *someone* - to live for.

Frustrated, my father spun away from me and continued searching the room. Inspecting every crevice, every nook. Dad was determined to find me out, and I was terrified of the repercussions if he found anything.

He started moving towards my bed, where I normally stored my bottles of vodka.

Shit.

In a display of his strength, he upturned the mattress.

He really was getting desperate.

He really wanted to find some booze.

"Hey," I objected, but a sharp look from him silenced me.

Dad sniffed around under my bed, the vein on his forehead pulsating like an overfilled pipe about to explode.

But he found nothing.

I breathed a sigh of relief.

Dad stood still, his anger subsiding. He didn't know what to do. He clearly came in my room expecting to catch something, to find me guilty. He didn't. And now he didn't know where to channel his frustration.

"Are you going to help me clean this up?" I asked him snidely, gesturing at my overturned mattress.

He also *didn't* like that comment.

He faced me, growling. Ignoring the bed. "How's school going, boy? You working hard?"

"Yes."

"You better. You know what'll happen if you fuck up again."

"I *know*. You don't need to repeat it."

"Remember it, boy. Remember what'll happen."

"Yep."

"If I catch you with a *single* bottle, or if you get into another fight, you know *exactly* where you're going."

"Where? Afghanistan or Iraq?"

Dad slithered back up to my face again. "I've had it with your sneers. You're *so* close. One more thing, one more step out of line, and you're out of here. You get me?"

"Crystal clear."

He marched out of my room, slamming the door behind him. I quickly locked it when he left. I didn't want him coming back in anytime soon.

I could act all tough and talk back to Dad, but he still frightened the *hell* out of me. I knew his threats were real. He really was ready to send me packing for the military. All it would take was for me to slip up again.

And I didn't plan on slipping up.

I wasn't planning to get into a fight so close to graduation.

Nope. I wasn't going to join the Army. Not this close to freedom.

I turned back to my upturned bed and sighed at the sight of it. I wasn't ready to fix it.

Screw Dad.

Instead of cleaning it up, I walked over to my shelf instead, catching a glimpse outside my window at Abby's house.

She was the one good thing in my life, and I needed to

keep her in it somehow. I'd been thinking about it all week, and I decided I was going to ask her to Prom. I was going to ask her out. Properly. A proper date, not just a coffee shop. Even though I detested high school and its social hierarchy and its popularity politics, I was still going to ask her to Prom. I was going to show her how much I cared about her the most public way I knew how.

I was going to ask her tonight.

Bite the bullet.

But first I needed a little bit of Dutch courage.

I found my Bible on my bookshelf. I pulled it out and opened it. Inside, I had hidden a bottle of whisky.

It was a good thing I decided to hide this in the one place I knew Dad wouldn't look.

It was time to ask Abby Starr to the Prom.

16

I was lying in my bed, late into the evening, when I heard the noise.

Thud.

It was like a bang. And it came from next door.

Serenity's room.

I immediately leaped out of bed, rushing to my door, rushing down the hallway, rushing into my sister's room.

I swung open her bedroom door, and that's when I saw her.

She was writhing around on the floor, having clearly fallen off her bed. Her eyes were rolled back in her head. Her hands were shaking. She was practically foaming at the mouth. She was unconscious.

Fuck.

I sprinted over to her and kneeled by her side.

It was her medical condition. She mustn't have taken her pills that night.

How could I have forgotten to tell her?

But I knew it was not the time to think about why. I had to help her. Urgently. I snatched her pillow off her bed and positioned it under her head to keep her from banging against the ground. I loosened her top to help her breathe. I pushed her cupboard away, making sure she couldn't bang against any sharp corners.

She needed help. She needed to get to the hospital.

I didn't need to be a qualified doctor to know this was serious.

I sensed someone enter the room behind me. Cameron. I spun around to him.

"Help me," I said, out of breath. "She needs to get to the hospital."

I watched on as my stepdad took in the situation, his beady eyes focusing on my sister shaking on the floor of her bedroom right in front of him.

"She's fine," he said. "Give her a minute."

"Give her a minute?" I asked, my mouth hanging open. I was in disbelief.

I spotted Mom standing behind my stepdad, peeking over him into the room. Surely, she could see something was wrong?

But no. She remained silent.

"She'll be alright in a second if you stop being so hysterical," Cameron said, shaking his head at me.

I couldn't believe it.

I turned back to my sister, softly rubbing my hand over her face to wipe off the spit that had gathered around her mouth. She was not okay. She needed medical help. What was happening wasn't normal, and she needed to be treated.

I checked she was still breathing. She was.

Thank God.

"Give me your keys," I said to my stepdad, flicking back

round to him and my Mom standing gormlessly over my sister and me.

"No."

"I need to take Serenity to hospital. You can either help me drive there or you can pass me your keys. One or the other."

Cameron said nothing. My mom said nothing. They just stared at Serenity and me. My sister was still shaking. She really needed help, and I wasn't going to get it from the two adults in the house.

I knew I needed to take this into my own hands.

I launched from the bedroom towards the kitchen, brushing past both my stepdad and Mom. I sprinted down the hallway to the front of the house, eyes scanning the kitchen counter.

I knew Cameron's keys would be there, just where he usually left them. They were sitting on the counter by the door. I snatched them and headed back to Serenity's room.

"I'm taking her to the hospital," I said to my stepdad and Mom as they stood there in the doorway to my sister's bedroom, flashing the keys in my hands. "I'm asking you to please help me or to get out of my way. Your choice, but I need your help."

They did neither.

They just gawked aimlessly at me as I went into Serenity's room and struggled to pick her up, as if they were watching a riveting show on TV. I awkwardly carried my sister past them and towards the front door of the house, the keys balanced precariously in my hands as I stumbled down the hallway, trying not to drop her. They didn't even bother to help.

Screw them.

I had to do this all by myself.

We made it outside, to my stepdad's car. I fastened her

in the backseat, her seizure lightening, but she was still unconscious. I double-checked everything was okay with her, that she wasn't biting her tongue and she was still breathing. She was.

I hopped into the front seat. I barely knew how to drive. I hadn't got my license, but I knew enough. Cameron's car was automatic, which made things a *lot* easier. I turned on the ignition and started the vehicle.

It was only then I realized I had tears streaming down my face. In the panic of trying to help my sister, I hadn't even realized I was crying. Nor that I was barely able to breathe.

I took a moment to calm myself. It wouldn't help anything at all if I were to crash on the way to the hospital. I checked on my sister again through the rearview mirror.

We had to get to the hospital. Fast.

I put my foot down on the pedal and began to drive.

* * *

I sat in the back of the taxi, cradling my sister's head. Stroking her hair.

She was okay.

She was safe.

We were going home.

We had been at the hospital for a few hours, enough time for the doctors to check her over multiple times. Her seizure was close to being serious; if I hadn't driven her straight to the hospital then who knew what could've happened. I waited anxiously in the emergency department until the doctors reassured me she was okay and that could go home that same evening. It was past midnight when we left. We decided to get a taxi instead of driving Cameron's car home. He could go and fetch it in the morning.

"Don't you scare me like that again," I said to my sister as we rested in the back of the taxi, the lights of the town flashing past us. "You really scared me."

"I'm sorry," she muttered, her voice soft as she leaned on me. I pulled her hair away from her face and sighed.

"Why didn't you take your pills?"

Serenity was quiet for a moment. "Because I don't like them. I thought I could skip them one time."

"It wasn't right."

"I know."

I wasn't going to pressure her or lecture her too hard. She'd been through hell. I was her big sister, not her mother. She didn't need me to tell her off, and certainly not now when she was still fresh from the hospital.

I kissed her forehead and snuggled my face against hers.

"I'm glad you're okay, sis," I whispered. "I love you."

"I love you too."

I never ever wanted to experience tonight again. Despite holding my sister tight in my arms and knowing she was safe; my heart rate was still racing and my breathing shallow. I was still in the lingering after stages of shock.

The taxi pulled up to the curb outside our house.

"Go inside," I said to my sister. "I'll pay the driver."

She scrambled out of the car and shuffled into the house. I took out a few notes and handed them to the driver, leaving him a tip.

I closed the taxi door behind me and took a moment for myself, breathing in the cool night air.

You need to calm down, Abby. Take your time.

I was worried about facing my stepdad and Mom again, and what I would say to them if I did.

To my left, someone emerged from the night shadows.

Miles.

Jesus.

I didn't want to see him. Not now. Not whilst I was still recovering from the night I just had. Not while my sister still needed comforting.

He stumbled towards me, and that's when I noticed he was drunk. He reeked of alcohol. I smelled in on his breath as he came towards me, his eyes shining in the darkness.

"Hello, Abby," he mumbled. "Long time, no see."

I shook my head at him. "Not now, Miles. I can't deal with anything at the moment."

"What's wrong?"

Tears stung at my eyes. It wasn't the first or even the second time I'd cried that night.

"Just... not now, okay? I can't talk to anyone right now."

But still, Miles kept advancing, swaggering closer until we were nearly touching. I could practically *taste* the alcohol on him.

"I need to ask you something," he slurred at me.

"You're drunk."

"I've had a drink. One drink. Or maybe a few."

"I'm not talking to you whilst you're drunk," I replied, and I meant it.

I faced away from him and started walking towards the front door of my house, but Miles wasn't giving up that easily.

"I need to talk to you, Abby," he said, voice rising.

"We can talk in the morning."

"No. Now."

I hushed him. "It's the middle of the night. What can possibly be the issue you want to talk to me about *right* now?"

"It's about school," he replied, swaying on his feet. He really was incredibly drunk. "It's about *Prom*."

Oh.

Fuck.

"Not now," I said, my voice struggling through the tears. I really couldn't deal with this right at that moment.

Couldn't he see the pain I was in or had his drink blurred even seeing that?

Miles reached out and grabbed my shoulder tightly. His fingers dug into my skin.

"I'm asking you out to Prom," he said, basically shouting in my face.

"My sister is inside," I replied. "We've just been to the hospital. She had a seizure. I really can't do this here."

A flash of recognition passed over Miles' eyes, but he still held on tight to me.

"Listen to what I'm saying," he said. "I'm asking you to Prom."

And that was the final straw.

I ripped his hand away from me and snarled at him. "Fuck off, Miles."

Couldn't he read the room? Couldn't he see what I was going through?

No. He was too blind drunk.

No one was prepared to help me. Not my stepdad, not my Mom, not even Miles. It was just my sister and me facing the world alone. We could only rely on each other, no one else.

Everyone lets you down.

Tears pouring down my face, I spun around and rushed inside, locking the door behind me.

That was it. He was drunk.

And I didn't want to see him ever again.

17

I APPLIED the finishing touches to my outfit. I watched myself in the mirror as I ran the red lipstick around my open mouth.

I puckered my lips together and carefully placed the lipstick down on the shelf with a flourish.

I nodded at myself in the mirror and blew out some anxious air.

The red dress I had on perfectly matched my lips and the red ribbon in my hair.

Okay. It looks good.

But now I needed to get a second opinion before I left that front door.

I left my room and hurried down the hallway into the living space. Serenity was lying on the couch balancing her head on her hands, watching TV. She sat up when I entered, checking me out up and down with wide, bewildered eyes.

"Abby," she said. "You look beautiful."

My cheeks flushed, and I smiled. "Thank you."

"Really, you do. Wow."

I twirled around in the dress.

"You think it's okay for Prom?" I asked nervously.

"Okay? It's more than okay. It's *perfect*. You look beautiful. You're going to be the prettiest girl there tonight." Serenity dived off the couch and scrambled past me, calling out as she headed into her room. "Wait a second. Let me get a photo of you."

I didn't exactly *want* to be going to Prom. I didn't really care to sort of just... stand around for a few hours and get drunk secretly from the teachers. I wasn't in a mood to dance. If it wasn't for Charlotte pestering me so much to come, then I wouldn't even be going. I just wanted the night to get over with quickly.

Not long until graduation.

She came back eagerly, carrying her phone. She stood by the doorway and flashed the camera at me. I smiled and tried to pose, sticking my tongue out for comical effect. Serenity took dozens of photos. She dashed to me to show them on the little screen.

Yep, she's right. I do look goddamn beautiful.

"Thanks, Serenity."

She looked up at me. I knew what she was thinking. I was thinking the same.

"I wish Dad could've seen you," she said.

Yep. Just what I was thinking.

"I know. Me too."

I didn't want to cry and ruin my makeup, so I turned away from Serenity's sad face.

I wished Dad were there. He could've taken me to Prom. He would've been so happy to see me dressed up like this. I could imagine his beaming smile.

Now I had no one.

"How are you going to get there?" my sister asked.

"I'll call a cab," I replied, fishing in my purse for my phone.

No one had asked me out for Prom. Well, except Miles. The other night. The night of Serenity's seizure and the night I told him to fuck off.

And he did. I hadn't seen him for the past few days, not since that night he drunkenly proposed to take me to Prom. What was he thinking? Did he really expect me to say yes when he was staggering around like that and slurring his words?

He hadn't been at school. I hadn't seen him on my trips to work. It was like he'd disappeared off the face of the earth.

He was like that. Unreliable.

But still. It would've been nice to have someone take me that night.

I found the taxi app and began to punch in what I wanted.

"I can take you there."

Both Serenity and I turned. It was Cameron. My stepdad had emerged from the hallway and was standing behind me.

"Pardon?"

"I can drive you there if you'd like," my stepdad said, shrugging.

"Really?" I asked, suspicious. It was very unlike Cameron to be kind like this. To act this generously.

"Yeah," he replied. "I have nothing else to do. I can drive you to the venue."

I glanced back at my phone, at the taxi app. Sure, it would be a lot cheaper and easier if Cameron just drove me there instead of hiring a taxi. Maybe he wanted to do a good deed before I left home forever?

Maybe this was his strange way of apologizing after his inaction the other night when I needed him to help me with Serenity?

"You sure?" I asked.

"Yep."

I checked back on my sister. She didn't seem to have any objections.

Yeah, this would make things a whole lot easier.

"Okay," I replied. "Thanks."

He snatched his keys from the kitchen counter and gestured for me to leave first. I gave a short hug to Serenity.

"You really do look beautiful," she whispered in my ear as she wrapped her arms around me. "Have a fun night."

I left the house and hopped into the front seat of my stepdad's car.

"Thanks again for doing this," I said as he settled in beside me in the driver's seat.

"No problem," he replied. "I think it's the least I can do."

"Well, thank you."

He didn't start the engine. "Abby, about the other night. With your sister..."

"It's okay," I said, waving away his concerns. "It's the past."

I really didn't need to have this awkward conversation with him. I was happy to just drop it.

"I should've helped you."

"It's okay."

He turned to me then, still having to start the car. Both of us inside it, sitting on the driveway. "You do look very beautiful tonight," he whispered. I felt him focusing in on me. On my body.

"Thank you."

"I've always found you very beautiful," he continued,

leaning in closer towards me. Closer than he'd ever been. "Very, very beautiful."

I shuffled over in my seat, away from him. "Thanks," I mumbled.

"Maybe you should forget about Prom," he hissed. "Maybe you should just stay with me."

Cameron reached out and wrapped his fingers around my hand. His cold skin against mine made me shiver with dread.

"Don't touch me," I said quietly. I was frozen in fear. I was stuck in a car with him. I pulled myself away even further, so that I was rubbing against the car door.

"What are you afraid of?" Cameron asked. "We can have fun together, you and me."

"No," I said, weakly. The sounds caught in my throat. I looked out of the car window. It was night outside. Darkness. No one could see us. No one could hear us. No one could help me.

He leaned even closer so that his lips were an inch away from mine. It was like his whole body had slithered over me, almost pinning me in the car.

"We could fuck," he whispered, smiling darkly. "We could do it in here and no one would know."

"I don't want this," I said, struggling against his grip. "Get off me."

"Come here," he said, and I began to feel his hand crawl up my arm.

"Stop it," I yelled. "No!"

I ripped my arm away from his grasp and unlocked the car door. I tumbled to the ground, my dress making contact with the grass. I didn't care about how messy I was, or even if I fell into mud, I needed to get away from him. I needed to escape.

I pushed myself off the hard ground and began to run

away from the car, but it was practically impossible. I couldn't run in the grass with my high heels. I didn't have the time to take them off.

I was stuck, slowly and pathetically trying to sprint away from the car.

I twisted my head to look back. Cameron had emerged from the car and was coming straight for me. His mouth turned into a satisfied grin.

The street was dark. There was nowhere I could go. No way I could get far in that dress and high heels.

I turned back around again. My stepdad was so close. He was taking his time, enjoying this chase.

I was screwed.

He would catch up to me in a few more seconds. He could have his arms around my face, muffling my screams in just a moment.

And then, as I watched, a dark shadow flew out of nowhere and collapsed into Cameron. Tackling him to the ground. I looked on in horror.

But the shadow wasn't anything supernatural. It wasn't a ghost. It was a man.

It was Miles Hunter.

He'd come out of nowhere and had grappled Cameron to the ground, pinning my stepdad to the grass. I saw Cameron's face full of surprise and terror.

And then Miles' arms were swinging in the night.

He was punching. Hitting Cameron in the face.

He was on top of my stepdad, beating the shit out of him. His legs trapped Cameron to the ground, and he leaned over my stepdad. A perfect position to aim for his face.

There was barely any sound beyond the whacks and thuds of Miles' fists crashing into Cameron's head. My stepdad stood no chance. My neighbor was wild. Frenzied.

"Stop," I said. "Please stop, Miles."

He didn't. He continued laying into my defenseless stepdad. I think I saw blood, but it was hard to tell in the darkness. There was so much movement.

It was like Miles was a pro at this.

My neighbor wasn't stopping. He wasn't giving up.

"Stop!" I screamed this time, unbalanced in my high heels.

And Miles did. His fists uncurled. He froze to the spot.

My stepdad groaned.

Miles had stopped.

Because of me.

18

ABBY

I COULDN'T BREATHE. My dress was constricting. My hands grabbed my waist as I struggled for breath. My throat dried and everything darkened.

I gasped for air.

I couldn't believe what had happened. One minute I was going to Prom, then Cameron was grabbing me in the car, then I was being chased by him across our yard, and then Miles had appeared out of nowhere to beat him up.

It all was so fast.

I staggered back on the grass, uneasy with my feet in high heels, as I tried to gulp in a lungful of air. I was falling. The world swam around me in slow motion. I knew I was falling, but I couldn't do anything to stop it.

Suddenly, arms were around me. Comforting arms.

Miles' arms.

He grabbed me before I could fall to the ground, gripping me tight to him. In his embrace, I found myself slowly able to breathe again. Slowly able to gasp in air. I felt my body shiver.

"You okay?" Miles asked me calmly, as if he hadn't just spent the last thirty seconds punching my stepdad on the ground only yards away.

I blinked up at him. I could see the outline of his face in the dark. The sharp strong edges of his jaw. His blue eyes shining in the moonlight. He looked concerned, even though he was the one who'd just been in a fight. One-sided, though it was.

My attention turned away from him. To the body lying on the grass.

My stepdad.

"Is he... dead?" I asked, my voice raspy.

The body on the grass groaned.

Miles smiled and shook his head. "Nope. No way near, but I bet he's going to wake up with a pretty shit headache in the morning."

Okay. Good.

I was glad he wasn't dead. I was glad Miles hadn't beaten him too badly.

But still, the man was unconscious.

"Where were you?" I asked my neighbor, still in his arms. I couldn't get the words out. "How... why?"

He laughed as if I were a child asking a silly question. "I was in my room drinking. I heard something going on. I saw what was going on. I had to help."

"So, you saw everything?"

He nodded. "Yeah."

I glanced back to my stepdad lying on the grass.

"Should we do something about him?" I asked.

"Like what?"

"Take him inside?"

"Why? Why would we do that? What he tried to do with you was unbelievable. Unforgivable."

"He might need help."

"He isn't going to die or anything," Miles replied. I could see in his eyes he was unrepentant. "Maybe a night out on the grass like this will do him good."

I pulled myself off Miles so that I was standing again. My knees were weak, and I swayed on the grass. My neighbor reached out and steadied me with a hand.

"You mentioned you were drinking?" I asked once I fully regained my balance.

"Yep."

"Well, I need a drink."

* * *

"So, you saw what happened from here?" I asked, peering out of Miles' window. I could see right across the yard that separated our two houses. I could see my window. So, this was where he was spying on me all this time?

"Yep."

"What were you doing?"

Wrapping his bruised knuckles in bandages by his desk, Miles coyly turned away from me. "I was actually writing you a letter."

"A letter?"

"Yep."

Oh.

"Can I see it?"

Miles chuckled softly and offered me a bottle of vodka. He was avoiding my question. "Drink?"

I took it from him and gulped a large sip without even thinking. The fiery liquid shot down my throat.

"That's just what I needed," I replied. "Thanks."

"No problem."

We had just climbed into his room from outside. I was afraid of Miles' parents finding out what we were doing.

What even are we doing?

I patted down my dress. Thankfully, it hadn't got too messy in my escape from my stepdad. It wasn't nearly as muddy as I'd thought it would be, but it was still ruined. I couldn't go out wearing something like this.

I guess I won't be going to Prom, then.

I still couldn't get my head around what had just happened, and what I would need to do now. Cameron was still outside between our two houses, unconscious.

One thing was for sure, though. In the morning, I was going to get out of that house somehow. No way was I ever staying there again.

And I would have to find a way to get my sister out as well.

I took in a deep breath and steadied myself. I was safe now. Here with Miles. I felt secure with him, and that was what I needed right then.

"So," I said to Miles. "How about that letter? Are you going to show it to me?"

"No."

I stretched over to place the vodka bottle on his desk when I saw it. The piece of paper with his handwriting on it. The letter. I moved to grab it, but Miles got to it first.

Damn.

"Let me have a read," I said cheekily.

"Nope."

I reached for it in his hand, and in response, Miles raised it in the air over his head. Out of my reach.

"Hey, that's not fair," I exclaimed, reaching for it. "I'll like to read it."

Miles laughed and kept his arm above him, knowing that my fingers couldn't lunge that far. "No."

"*Please?*"

"No." Miles laughed again. It was my chance. He dropped his hand just low enough for me to be able to snatch the piece of paper from him.

I rushed to the window and unfurled it, reading the words quickly before he had a chance to take it back.

DEAR NEIGHBOR,

I don't know what to write but sorry for the other night. I was an idiot. I hope you can forgive my stupid drunk ass.

IT WASN'T FINISHED. It was obvious he was still writing it when he saw what was happening to me in the car opposite his window.

But I understood what he was trying to say.

He was sorry.

Wow.

I wiped a tear away from my face and turned to Miles. He stood there, in the middle of the room, his head bowed.

"I truly am sorry," he said softly. "I hope your sister is alright. I should've listened to you, but I was so self-involved I didn't. I've been beating myself up for the last few days. I haven't slept. I haven't eaten."

I rushed up to him and wrapped my arms around him. His body was warm against mine.

"I'm sorry too," I said. "The other night was... crazy. My sister had been in hospital and my head was in a lot of places. I wasn't thinking straight. I shouldn't have told you to fuck off."

He laughed. I felt his hot breath against my ear. "You had every reason to tell me to fuck off."

"That's the last thing I want you to do."

He pulled me away from him, holding me by the shoulders. We stared at each other's eyes. Growing closer.

I didn't know who leaned forward first, or if we did it together, but soon enough, we were kissing.

And it was perfect.

He held me in his arms as his lips grazed mine. I was soft, and he pressed into me, and then our bodies touched. He was all around me. My hands traveled up to his long, blonde hair. I ran them through the strands, pulling him even closer to me.

I had a taste of him, and it wasn't enough to satisfy me. I wanted more.

His lips were tender but torching. I felt him deep within

me. My heart seemed to burst out of my chest as he touched me.

He was not a boy, but a man.

And I knew he wanted me.

"You can have me," I told him, as if I could read his mind. I practically could. I knew him so well.

"Yeah?" It was a moan from him, barely a coherent word.

"Yes," I replied, gasping for air. "You can have all of me."

And so. He did.

Miles lifted me in the air, my dress billowing out around him like a cape, and then he brought me to his bed. I fell upon his mattress with a giggle as Miles began to tear away at me, wanting to undress me like he was hungry for my body.

"No," I said, swatting away his greedy hands. "You first."

Miles hissed, then smiled. He stood up from the bed and flung his leather jacket off. Then, with one hand, he pulled up his shirt over his head in such a sexy way my body began to pulsate with desire. His skinny body was all edges and cliffs. Abs and muscles. No fat at all.

He was simply *gorgeous*.

He noticed how I drank him in with my eyes.

"You like what you see?" he asked.

"How could I follow up when you look *so* good?" I replied.

Miles bit his lower lip and sighed. "Let me have a look at you, then. So I can decide for myself."

I fulfilled his request, and soon I was out of my dress. Completely naked. My tits hard for him.

"I like what I see," Miles said, scanning me in up and

down as he undid his belt, letting his tight jeans fall to his ankles.

The bulge under his underpants made my eyes wide.

He was so big.

So hard. For me.

With a single finger, he pulled down the hem of his underpants and his cock sprung out. All the inches of it. Thick and veiny. Pre-cum glistening on the tip.

I gulped, fully realizing that, in a few moments, I would no longer be a virgin. That he would be inside me. And I loved it.

My pussy throbbed with heated desire. I was ready for him.

I wanted him.

But instead of going straight for me with his engorged cock, Miles smiled, and then I felt the tip of his finger start to circulate around my wet sex. I let off a gasp as I felt him play with me. Teasing me in the parts he knew where to make me feel the most pleasure. Filling me with tension as his finger traced the outline of my eager pussy.

I jerked and moaned. "Please, Miles," I begged. "Please get inside me."

"No."

His movements grew faster. He knew *exactly* what to do. He played me like a fiddle. I was dazed, but elated. My hips moved in rhythm to his hand, pushing him along, helping him force me to reach climax.

My hands stretched for his, and my nails dug into his skin as I swelled more and more intense. I couldn't hold it back anymore.

I needed him. I really, really needed him.

And, as I reached breaking point, he slipped away from me.

"*Please*," I begged. No way could he tease me like that and then leave. I didn't want him to go.

I lifted my head to see him wrap a condom around his shaft and I fell back onto his mattress, brimming with excitement. I knew what was coming next, and I was more than ready for it.

I didn't have to wait for long. I felt the head of his cock kiss against the outline of my pussy, tenderly preparing me for what was about to occur.

I was going to be a virgin no longer.

"You want me?" Miles asked.

I nodded greedily. "Yes."

"You *really* want me?"

"Please."

And then he entered me.

I arched my back and let out a soft moan as I felt the sheer size of his cock feed deep inside me. Miles' hands reached up to my tits and squeezed gently. My nipples responded to his grip, growing even more erect. I felt him inside me, all of him. I closed my eyes, unable to control myself no longer. I just had to have him inside me.

I forgot all about that night. All of it except for one thing. Miles' blue eyes shining in the moonlight. The way he caught me when I fell. How he put me first above everything else, including his own safety.

Delicately, Miles thrust in and out, forcing me to move in time with his body like we were one. My hands grabbed hold of his face, tracing his perfect jawline with the tips of my fingers. His lips were pink and wet. He pushed his own finger into my mouth, and I sucked at it hungrily. His finger muffled my moans as he continued to thrust inside me, filling me with his large cock.

Miles moved into a steady rhythm and I rocked with him.

"You're beautiful," he whispered in the dark.

That was all I wanted to hear. What I'd been dying to hear from him for so long.

"So are you," I moaned through his finger as he dug in further deep inside me with both his hand in my mouth and his cock in my pussy. I was so wet for him, so *open*.

This is what sex feels like?

I didn't want it to end.

Not when it was with Miles. My gorgeous neighbor.

Miles had fought off my stepdad. He'd tenderly touched me. He protected me. This act we were doing together was like a cleansing. Like I was forgiving him. This was the best way I could say I *wanted* him.

He fucked me hard. Riding me deeply. His hips worked vigorously into me.

And then I was letting go. My whole body shook as a great purge of warmth burst out of my pussy. I was high on Miles. My finger quivered and my eyes rolled into the back of my head as I cried out in ecstasy.

I'd thought about this moment so many times, when I was alone, when I was in a shower. I'd thought what it'd be like to climax like this.

And here I was *doing* it.

Miles leaned over me, having thrust deep inside. He grunted as I moaned.

I felt his lips on mine as we both reached the tip of sex. Hot air pushing forth from his mouth. He held me tight and muttered my name as he came and I climaxed.

"Abby. *Abby*."

And I whispered back.

"Miles. *Miles*."

19

ABBY

MILES PULLED ME IN TIGHTER, his manly hairy leg draping over my body. I was fully enmeshed with him. Stuck in his tight embrace on top of his bed.

And I didn't want to leave.

It was early the next morning, only a few hours since my next-door neighbor had rescued me from my crazy step-dad. A few hours since he apologized to me. A few hours since I lost my virginity. We both lay in his bed, wrapped in his sheets and each other. Smelling of each other and the hot sweaty sex we'd just had.

And I loved it.

Yep. I really didn't want to leave.

I turned my head to face Miles. He lay face-up, staring at the ceiling, a spare hand of his nonchalantly stroking my hair over and over on the same strand. He was thinking. He appeared so cute, his full lips slightly pouting and his blue eyes glaring aimlessly upwards. I kissed the sharp edge of his square jaw.

"Thank you for that," I cooed softly.

He slowly snapped out of his daydream, the corners of his lips turning into a smile.

"Thank *you*," he whispered back, still looking up at the ceiling.

I watched him for a moment longer, one hand over his heart, feeling his muscular chest gradually rise and fall in an unbroken rhythm.

"You know, I've just lost my virginity."

"I know."

"I wanted to lose it to you."

He turned to me then, his blue eyes resting on mine. "I know."

He must've felt my heartbeat stop when he said that. We were so entangled with each other; he must've known how my body reacted to his words.

"What's going to happen to us?" I asked, my voice beginning to break.

"What do you mean?"

"Our future."

"You mean once we graduate?"

I nodded. "Yeah."

Miles sighed. "I dunno, but whatever happens, I want you beside me."

For the second time in a matter of minutes, my heart stopped again.

"I would like that."

He continued speaking softly. "It's like there's a path, and we've come to a fork in the road. But, instead of two different paths to go down, there's a million. I guess that's what the end of school is really, the one moment in life where there are a million different paths to choose from."

"I see that too."

"I just hope to choose the right one," he said, sighing.

"How will you know if you have?" I asked, and Miles smiled at me again.

"If it has you in it," he replied. "Then I'll know if I've chosen the right one."

I leaned up and kissed his lips. "Me too," I said.

"At the very least, we should still write to each other."

"Yeah," I replied. "No matter what."

"No matter what."

PART 2

20

Dear Neighbor,

It happened last week. And even though it happened so recently, I can barely remember it at all.

I remember little things. They come back to me like snippets in my mind. Kind of like when you skip through a film you're watching and there are just, like, random images of it taken every ten seconds, but there's still enough to kind of understand the narrative. You get what I mean?

I'm rambling again like I always do. Typical me.

But yeah. The thing. It happened last week. We were driving, that I can remember. There was sand, loads of it. Fucking hot sand. And it was everywhere, but that isn't much of a surprise though, isn't it? You should expect that there's sand out here, but even then, I'm still mind blown by how fucking much there is. It really gets everywhere.

We were driving. I think we were talking, or we were listening to music. We were doing something. I can't recall what. Out here, it seems like all we do is talk shit or listen to crap rock from the eighties. But it isn't important what we were doing.

Then there was an almighty crash. It was like there'd

been an earthquake or something. Something really big, you know? It felt like the world was exploding. Then there was lots of sand blowing all around. As if there wasn't enough already.

I fucking hate the sand here.

I remember seeing the ground. I was on the ground. Which I remember thinking was super weird, because I was sitting in the back of a vehicle just moments before. But now I was outside. I remember accidentally looking into the sun. I remember checking that all my limbs were there.

But then that's when my memory starts to fucking deteriorate.

I think I remember crawling, or I might be imagining it. I've seen someone about this in the last week, some therapist or psychologist or whatever they're called. I wasn't too keen, but I didn't have much choice but to visit them. They said that it's common I have blackouts during an experience like that. They said that sometimes you might even make up shit that didn't happen. Maybe that's true, so don't take everything I write as the Gospel, okay?

But I definitely remember making it, somehow, to my friend. He's called Curtis, by the way. I don't know if I've written about him before. Curtis was lying face-down in the sand. That fucking sand again. Somehow, I pulled him over and removed his stuff. I don't really remember that, but I must've done it. He was practically naked.

But then I was carrying him.

The rest of it goes by in a crazy blur. This is when things get really rocky in my mind, but people have said I carried him a couple of miles or so back to civilization. I don't know how far. But that's what happened, and I don't even remember any of it.

I don't even know why I'm writing this all down to you. You'll probably think I'm crazy. Reading this back, it just *seems like a jumble of words. I dunno. It's supposed to help, isn't it? Writing things down.*

That's what the fucking therapist says. I really don't know.

We'll see if it helps me.

21

ABBY

"Is that going to be bottle or draught?" I asked Kevin, my arm resting on the beer tap.

"You know what I like," Kevin grumbled back at me, pulling a frown. He sat in his usual place, on a stool right by the side of the bar. The best place to moan constantly at us bartenders.

And that was what he was doing again. For the fifth night in a row. Now it was time to give him a little bit of his own medicine.

"I don't know your drink of choice, no. And neither do you, it seems," I replied with a big grin on my face. I was enjoying teasing the man. "What with your dementia and all."

"Hey, I'm not that old," he barked back.

"Seems like it," Sonia, my fellow bartender, replied with a smirk as she poured a beer for another customer, listening in on Kevin and my interaction.

"Hey, girls," my customer squawked. "Show me some

respect here."

I laughed. "You mean, like, *respect your elders*?"

"No," Kevin replied, pressing one of his fingers into his chest proudly. "Respect your customers."

"Kevin," I said. "You're no customer. If you spent any longer here, then you'll start receiving paychecks. You practically work here with all the time you're here at the bar."

"Plus, your tab is pretty deep in the red," Sonia butted in and I nodded at her remark.

"Kevin, let's face it," I continued. "You ain't no customer, and I'm certainly not going to respect you."

The old man grumbled again, something about *the youth of today*, but I knew he enjoyed our little spat. Our dirty back and forth were the main reason why Kevin continued returning to O'Malley's Bar every night I worked there, which was basically every night of the week. He liked to flirt foul with me and, as long as he kept handing me the generous tips he tended to give out, I liked to flirt equally nasty back. I knew how to hold my own in such a dive as O'Malley's and the kind of seedy customers we attracted.

And *boy*, was the place a dive. O'Malley's was a cheesy old Irish bar. Smack bang in the middle of downtown, but really only serving old regulars like Kevin; the place fitted the very cliché of a watering hole only alcoholics and those on that particular path would want to drink in. With the stale beer stench of the place and the dim unwelcoming lighting, we occasionally had a few tourists poke their noses inside for a drink. They would usually take one look at the place, with the tawdry Irish flags hanging from every available corner to the crap American liquor we served behind the beer-stained bar, and promptly would make their leave. I couldn't blame them. I would never step into a place like O'Malley's unless it was where I had to work.

And I did work there. All the time. Twenty-four-seven, it felt like some weeks. Like I was serving a prison sentence.

So, *yeah*, I could dish it out to the alcoholics who loved a bit of bite to their bartender and sometimes a slap to my ass as I passed. With those guys, I usually taught them a lesson or two and they'd either leave or never touch me again.

But, as long as the tips kept flowing, then I didn't mind too much. I was working there for one thing and one thing only.

Making money.

"How about I buy you a drink?" Kevin asked me as Sonia handed him his beer.

Behind the bar, I folded my arms and looked him square in the eye. He looked like a guy who'd never touched a glass of water before in his life. He looked like the kind of guy who'd come out of his mother's womb sucking on a bottle of Budweiser. Red, papery skin. Thinning hair. A big round belly. He looked like any one of our usual regulars who provided most of O'Malley's income with their steady demands for more beer down their throats.

"You know you can't do that," I replied.

He laughed, trying to test me. He wasn't going to get far. "And why not?"

"You know perfectly well, Kevin. Stop playing games."

"Right, you *don't* drink." He said that like it was an impossible idea. Like no one else in the entirety of human history had ever decided not to drink alcohol. Like I was insane.

"You can buy me a Coke," I replied, and Kevin waved a fat arm at me.

"Pah."

I smiled back. I fluttered my eyelashes at him and pouted. "Please buy me a Coke," I said in a high-pitched baby voice. "Please, mister big man."

Kevin knew when I was mocking him, but he enjoyed the show, nonetheless.

"I don't buy non-alcoholic drinks, sweetheart," he replied. "But here's a tip for you to save towards your implants. Maybe if you get some big ones, then you'll find a guy to buy you a Coke."

He handed me a twenty-dollar bill. I took the folded note from him and slipped it between my breasts. Kevin watched on. Horny.

"Thanks, big boy," I replied.

I didn't know how much the old customer and I were actually kidding around now, but hey, it was free money. Money that I could use for Serenity. Money that might mean more textbooks for her, and that was only a good thing.

"Abby?" I heard someone calling for me from behind.

Sonia whispered in my ear. "It's Trevor."

I grunted back at her.

Great. Not him.

I winked at Kevin before I turned away from him. "Adios."

"Abby?" Trevor called again from behind the bar. I rolled my eyes.

"Yeah, yeah. I'm coming."

It was Trevor, my boss. Manager of O'Malley's and its number one douchebag. He stood around the corner, out of sight of the bar's customers at the doorway into his office. I walked around the bar and glared at him.

"What, Trevor? I'm busy working out there."

"Come," he said, beckoning me inside the office with a curl of a finger. I hated being treating like that, like as if I were a naughty schoolgirl going into the principal's office. I was twenty-two, far too old for such power games as what Trevor was playing.

He was only a few years older than me, but being made manager of the cheesy Irish bar had gone to his head and he'd developed some kind of dictator syndrome. Lording it over the rest of us waitresses. Trevor acted like this bar was his kingdom, and I was just some courtier he hired to use my youthful female body to entertain the guests. I mean, *yeah*, that was practically what I was hired to do, but he didn't have to be such a dick about it.

He brought me into his office and settled down in the sole chair in the room, leaving me to stand awkwardly. Yep, this was some *small dick* power dynamic he was trying to impose in there. I waited for him to speak first. I just wanted to leave and get back into doing my job.

"You need to stay longer tonight, Abby."

That's what he's opening with?

Great managerial strategy there. Very *inspiring*.

"Why?" I asked.

"Gabriella's called in sick. We're short-staffed. We need an extra pair of hands for tonight."

"My shift ends at seven." I glanced at the clock on the office wall. "That's in an hour."

My manager rolled his eyes and lifted his feet to rest on top of his desk. Yeah, real power moves there. "I know that," he said. "But you need to stay longer."

"Not tonight, Trevor."

"And why not?"

"I have errands to run."

"What errands?"

"Why should I tell you?" The man remained silent, staring at me. I sighed. I knew I wouldn't be leaving the office until he had an answer. I just wanted to work out the rest of my shift, collect my tips, and leave. Trevor would make it difficult if I didn't respond. "Fine. I need to get to the pharmacy before it closes."

"Why?"

"Do you really need to know that?"

"Yep."

This wasn't going anywhere. I was not going to work late. That was final. "My sister has a... condition. She needs to get her medication in time. I need to collect it on the way home by tonight and I can't do that if I leave here late and the place is closed."

Trevor bit his lip and scratched his chin, taking his time to reply. "Fine," he eventually said. "But you should know you're leaving us in the shit here."

"How about you go out and help on the bar? They could do with your help."

I don't think Trevor had actually served customers for a very long time. He preferred to lazy around the office in the back, picking his nose or masturbating or whatever he did. He thought he was above bar tending. Above the rest of us, now that he wore a manager's badge.

He chuckled. "Don't tell me how to do my job."

"Alright," I said. "Can I go?"

Without waiting for his answer, I turned to leave the office, but he barked across the room before I even made it to the doorway.

"One final thing, Abby."

"What is it?" I asked.

Trevor hadn't moved. His feet still sat up on his desk, a shit-eating grin spread out across his ugly face. "Don't flirt with the customers."

"Jealous, are we?"

"It's unprofessional."

"Look at the sign above the door," I replied to the manager sassily. "We're an Irish bar tucked away in one of the seediest parts of the city, Trevor, not a fine dining establishment. How else do you think us girls make the money that goes into your salary?"

He was rendered wordless by my comeback. He opened and closed his mouth. No reply coming from the douchebag, it was the best time for me to saunter out of there and back to the bar to wait out the rest of my shift. He was only jealous because I didn't flash my tits in his face and let him have his way with me like some of the other, more desperate waitresses had to in order to get a little money on the side to pay the bills.

And I didn't plan to do so.

I flirted with the customers for tips, but I would never do so with Trevor.

I headed back to the bar, poured Kevin another beer, and waited out the rest of my shift; my mind focused entirely on getting Serenity's medication in time.

22

ABBY

I'D JUST GOT into the apartment building, gripping in one hand the keys to my apartment and in the other the bag of pills for Serenity I'd just got from the pharmacy when I saw the beam of light from the open door of my neighbor's apartment.

My next-door neighbor's door was ajar.

That was unusual. It was late. Too late past the bedtime for Mr. Clarke - my next-door neighbor - a shy old retiree who largely kept to himself and, from what I'd gleaned from past conversations with him, was always happily tucked up in bed by nine. A perfect neighbor. He never made a sound.

So, what was he doing up so unusually late and why was his door open?

Whatever it is, it can't be good.

"Mr. Clarke?" I called out as I ascended the stairs to our level. The light from inside his apartment spilled out over the staircase. "Mr. Clarke, are you alright?"

There was no answer. The man was partially deaf, so maybe he couldn't hear me.

Or maybe something worse has happened.

"Mr. Clarke?" I hailed again, but still no answer. There was no movement from behind the door, no shadows lurking between the gaps.

I should check up on him. I should make sure he's okay.

Carefully, I approached his apartment, reaching my hand out to slowly push open the door further. Images of a burglar or someone sneaking around inside screamed in my mind as I peered around the opening in the doorway.

But what I saw was the opposite of what I was afraid of.

Mr. Clarke's apartment was not in shambles. It hadn't been ransacked or burgled. My eyes quickly adjusted to the bright light, and I made out the figure of Mr. Clarke standing on the far side of his living room, next to a towering pile of plain cardboard boxes.

He was okay.

"Mr. Clarke?"

The old man was startled by the sound of my voice. He jumped back and turned to me, sighing when he saw who it was that had surprised him.

"Oh, Abby," he said, advancing towards me in his doorway with a twinkle in his eye. "You gave me such a fright."

"Sorry, Mr. Clarke. I saw the door open..."

"And you assumed I had kicked the bucket?" My neighbor chuckled, amused at his own little joke.

"Well, not like that, Mr. Clarke. Nothing as dark as that," I replied, opening the door so that I was no longer leaning around it. "I just wanted to check what was going on."

"And does everything seem to be alright to you?"

"As long as you are, Mr. Clarke," I replied. He was in a

giddy mood. I nodded towards the pile of cardboard boxes. "What are all those?"

He turned and gestured at them. "I'm moving."

"*Moving?* As in leaving?"

"Yes, I've had enough of the city life."

That was a surprise.

"You've been living here for a long time, Mr. Clarke."

"Nearly thirty years," he replied. "But it's time for me to leave. It's time for me to head out to the country. I want to be near my grandchildren."

I patted his shoulder. "That's nice. I bet they'll love to see you more."

He winked at me. "Oh, they're going to be sick of me by the number of times I'll visit," he said.

"When do you leave?"

"Tomorrow. Apparently, the next tenant will be moving in straight away tomorrow afternoon, or so the estate agent told me."

My eyes widened. "Really? That's quick."

A new next-door neighbor? I wonder what they'll be like.

Probably nowhere as near as quiet as Mr. Clarke.

"I thought so too."

"I didn't even know there were showings," I said.

"There were some yesterday," my neighbor replied. That must've happened when I was working at O'Malley's. "The new tenant put down their deposit as soon as they saw the place."

"Wow. Really quick."

"I think they really wanted this place."

"Did you meet them?"

"No, it was the estate agent who told me all this."

"Wow," I repeated. "Thank you for letting me know, Mr. Clarke. I hope your moving goes well."

"Thank you," he replied, giving me a wink.

"Sorry for startling you."

I unlocked the door to my own apartment, heading inside with Mr. Clarke peeping from his doorway.

The TV was on in my place. My sister was lying on the couch, watching it intently. Our apartment was smaller than Mr. Clarke's. It was the tiniest in the whole building. It was all I could afford in the city for both my sister and me to live in, and even then, it took me over an hour just to reach downtown to go to work. That meant I left and came back from work exhausted just from the traveling.

But anything was better than my mom's house. Every morning I woke up in my cramped apartment, thankful that I was no longer under my mom's roof.

The place was confined and modest, but at least it was *mine*.

I dumped my work bag by the front door and collapsed onto the couch beside Serenity, throwing the container of pills I'd just got at her.

"Make sure you take them," I said before burying my face into a pillow. It had been a long day and an equally long shift at work. Trevor's constant power plays hadn't made it easier. "I just want to fall asleep and not wake up for a thousand years."

"You go ahead and do that," Serenity said. "I'll stay here and watch TV."

"And who'll pay for your lifestyle?"

"I'm sure I can find someone else to mooch off."

"Right."

It had been four years since I graduated and moved out of home, taking my sister along with me. We relocated to the city, and I adopted Serenity the first chance I took, trying to build up a life for her and me far away from the reach of our mom. And especially Cameron.

I flipped over on the couch and snuggled up against my sister.

"How about you turn the TV off and do your homework?" I asked. It was hard juggling being an older sister and having to act like a mom to her, but I was the only person in her life now. The only person who understood her struggles, both medically and with our insane family. I was the only person she could rely upon, and that meant sometimes having to act like a bitch to get her to do the things she needed to do.

"All done."

"What?" I asked. "You've completed all your homework?"

"Yep."

"Well, double-check it. It's important you get good marks. You need to get a good education."

"I know, I know," my sister replied. "You want me to get good marks so that I can move out of here and get out of your life."

"No, it's because I want you to have a good future, Serenity. I want you to be able to go to a good college, get a good job. Not end up working in some shit Irish bar like I do, getting your ass spanked by every trucker who passes through."

"Okay."

"Listen to me," I said, twisting to her so that we faced each other. "You don't want what I have to do every day, trust me. I only want what's the best for you."

"I just want *you*," Serenity replied softly. "I don't care about jobs or education. I just want to be with you."

God damn, she was really cute sometimes. How could I be expected to lecture that face?

I grabbed her hand and kissed the back of it. "You're too sweet for me, Serenity. You know that?"

"Well, maybe you can let me watch a bit more TV?"

I rolled my eyes and stood up from the couch. "Okay, just a little bit more. I'm off to bed. I'm so *freaking* tired from work."

"Is Trevor still a dick?" she asked as I headed towards the bedroom.

"He's not too bad," I replied. I'd confided in her numerous times about the... struggles at work.

"Abby, he *is* a dick. A big one."

"Shut up, you. Don't use that kind of language."

"You do."

"Well, when you're twenty-two, then you can speak whatever you like. Until then, you're under my roof. My roof, my rules."

My sister made a face at me and I laughed at her all the way into the bedroom.

I flicked on the light. We shared the room, our two beds sat at opposing walls.

I'd told my sister I was going to sleep, but I lied. I wasn't going to bed just yet.

Instead, I made sure the door was closed so that Serenity couldn't see me, then I leaned under my bed and checked for something.

Good. It was still there.

I pulled it out.

A small black box. A little safe.

Something I kept hidden from the rest of the world.

And, double-checking the coast was clear, I opened it.

23

ABBY

I sat down on my bed holding the little black safe. My hands reached for the necklace around my neck. At the end of it hung a key.

I slid the key into the safe's lock and carefully opened the black box as to not damage the contents within. They were delicate. Inside was a pile of thin papers.

They were all the letters Miles had written to me.

I unfolded the top letter in the box. It was the last letter he ever wrote to me.

The same letter I snatched from him the night he saved me from my stepdad. The same night I lost my virginity.

I read the uncompleted letter for what seemed to be the millionth time.

DEAR NEIGHBOR,

I don't know what to write but sorry for the other night. I was an idiot. I hope you can forgive my stupid drunk ass.

I HAD READ it so many times I had practically memorized the words on the page. I ran my fingers over his neat handwriting. The little curl in his *f*. He never did finish writing the letter. I stole it from him that night and kept it for myself before he could finish writing what he started. I didn't know then it would be the last time he ever wrote to me.

And that it would be the last time we would speak.

I'd kept all his letters, stored in that little black safe, for the past four years under my bed. No one else knew about them, not even Serenity. It was like a secret world existed in that safe among those delicate scraps of paper. A world frozen in time to that night Miles and I made love, a world existing only for me.

How I longed to go back. How I wished I could tell my past self to treasure every moment of that night inside Miles' bedroom.

Because little did I know, that would be the last time I ever saw him.

Thinking about Miles now made me angry. I stuffed the uncompleted apology letter back in the safe and slid it back under my bed, angry at myself for daring to bring up memories of him.

I knew I shouldn't have been thinking of him.

He fucked you once and then he disappeared. Stop romanticizing that asshole.

I didn't know what happened that night four years earlier. I didn't know what I must've done to send Miles packing. That night in his bed was the last time I ever saw him. I went home the next day to collect my sister and to escape my stepdad, and when I came back for Miles, he was gone. Disappeared off the face of the earth.

I went around to his place to talk, but his parents didn't answer the door. I even staked out in front of his bedroom window in hope of catching him unaware, but he was never there. It was like he never existed. Like he'd been a ghost. A figment of my imagination.

But I knew he was real.

Why would he evaporate like that? Was it because of me? What had I done to make him fly away?

I moved into a hostel with Serenity straight after that night. We needed to get out of that house and away from my stepdad. I never wanted him to go anywhere near my sister ever again. I stayed in that place for the last week of the school year. Right on up to graduation.

And then I moved to the city. I gave up on the hope of going to college to instead work full time at O'Malley's - first as a waitress and then as a bartender when I was old enough - to make sure Serenity had a shot at a decent life, a decent education, and to pay for her medication. I resolved to work in that bar unless something better came along or until Serenity entered adulthood and could go her own way.

Cameron and Mom, knowing I had left home, obviously didn't want the police involved and never filed a missing person's report. They never fought legally to get Serenity back. They never did care about her, about us. I never saw them again.

I was free.

But I still didn't know what had happened with Miles.

For the last few weeks of school, he never bothered showing up. It was like he was wiped clean from history.

No one would tell me where he'd gone. I was lost, consumed by thoughts of him.

Missing him.

Wondering where I went wrong.

I sat down on my last day in the hostel, the day before I moved permanently to the city, and I wrote him a letter. It was the last letter I ever sent to him. I wrote down my new address in the city. I told him to visit. I told him I didn't understand what had happened between us, but whatever it was, I was ready to forgive and forget.

I told him I loved him.

I sealed it in an envelope and sent it to his parents' house.

But I never received a reply.

I never did find out what happened to him.

It took me a long time to wipe the thoughts of him away from dominating my mind. I resigned myself to the lack of closure. Miles was a dick for abandoning me like that without a word, nothing more. Just another asshole guy breaking a girl's heart. A tale as old as time.

There were a million better ways he could've told me he no longer wanted me in his life instead of vanishing the way he did. But, *hey*. That's life. Men really are uncaring assholes.

You just had to learn to move on. I knew it was down to me, just like it had always been. I'd learned the hard way you couldn't rely on anyone in life. You had to do everything yourself.

Even mend your broken heart.

I kept his letters, though. That was my closure. I could store my thoughts and memories of him in that little black safe under my bed, taking him out of the darkness only when I wanted to. On my terms. I now had control over when I dreamed about him.

But he still made me angry.

I paced around the bedroom, trying to shake off the sense of Miles that lingered all over my body after reading that letter.

I knew I was still not over him, even after all these years.

He still had my heart.

The bastard.

24

ABBY

IT WAS a busy night at O'Malley's. I darted from one side of the bar to the other, pouring drinks and flicking open bottles for all the customers lined up against the counter.

"Next!" I called out. Some guy with the audacity to wear sunglasses indoors raised his hand, and I rushed over to him, leaning over the bar to better hear his order. The customers were ramming up against the counter. It was utter chaos.

Some big football game was on in the city. I didn't care much for sports. But it was bringing loads of people into O'Malley's, which obviously was good for business. I'd never seen the place so full in all the four years I'd worked there. The Irish bar was packed to the rafters, and not just the usual crazy old regulars either, but with actual *people* who weren't daytime alcoholics. People who were willing to hand out some good tips.

If there was ever a time to work hard, it was now.

I wiped sticky sweat off my brow with the back of my

hand as I poured another Bud for a waiting customer. I'd been running around on my feet for the last several hours without a single break. It seemed like I hadn't stopped moving since midday; we were that busy the entire time. Sonia and I rushed through the orders as they came in. We were good at serving. And at being a good team together.

Unlike Trevor.

Instead of helping us hurried waitresses with the relentless waves of customers, our manager sat in the office, his legs lazily propped up on his desk in the comfortable way he liked. He didn't leave that room in the back of the bar all day, preferring to sit around in there scratching his balls or whatever he did, whilst the waitresses and I sweated by the bucketloads, making sure every customer was served.

Making sure the money flowed in whilst Trevor sat back and reaped the rewards.

"Next!" I called out again. A man in a Hawaiian shirt propped himself halfway over the bar and beckoned a fat finger at me.

"Beer," he yelled, his big belly resting on the liquor-stained counter. A grotesque sight.

I nodded to him and turned to the fridge behind me, chuckling to myself. He was just another aggressive customer in a sea of them we'd had that day. I caught Sonia's eye as she passed me. She gave me a wink and a nod towards my Hawaiian shirt customer in solidarity. I winked back at her.

Even if it's a crazy day and we're dealing with an ocean of seedy nut jobs, at least we're working with each other.

Although we could've dealt with another pair of hands, Trevor preferred keeping his rested behind his head in his office.

Fucking great.

But I didn't have time to concern myself with our lazy-as-fuck manager; there were too many people to serve and not enough hands to open beers and take cash.

It was left to me to be in charge behind the bar, seeing as Trevor was busy doing nothing in the office and the fact that I was the longest-serving member of staff. And the eldest. I was informally in charge of a group of twenty-one-year-old waitresses on the busiest day of O'Malley's history.

But we made it through the night.

Just.

We survived. Barely intact, but all without any major fuck ups.

It was a *goddamn* miracle.

Our team of twenty-somethings all hugged when the last customer left and as we locked the doors in celebration of getting through the night.

"We'd made it," I said to the team. I'd really become the informal manager that night through blood, sweat, and tears. That's what counts in the hospitality industry, that's what earns you respect. Hard work. "Well done, guys."

We counted the tips and split them evenly whilst Trevor counted the tills in the office. He'd only emerged once that entire day, and that was to collect the cash to count it. It'd been left up to me to basically be the manager. All he was interested in was profit.

With the tips handed out, the waitresses all left, leaving me alone in O'Malley's amongst the cheap Irish decorations and beer-stained floor.

I pulled a beer from the fridge and drank it, propping myself on the bar's counter. I barely drank alcohol usually, and I certainly didn't let customers buy me a drink, but I think I deserved that beer. I took in a deep breath and sighed.

Yeah, it'd been a very long day.

But good tips.

That was something.

Trevor emerged from his office. I glanced over at him as he leaned over the bar next to me.

"We're down," he said, his voice low.

"What do you mean?" I asked.

"We're down by a few hundred bucks."

"Really? How much did we make, though?"

"Over ten grand, but that doesn't matter. We're down by nearly two hundred dollars."

I took a sip of the beer and thought about it for a moment. "Ten grand. That's a lot."

It was the most O'Malley's ever made in a single day since I'd been there.

"Yes," Trevor replied darkly. He was frowning. "We're still missing a few hundred."

"It's probably an accumulation of mistakes, Trevor," I explained. "We were crazy busy today."

"That's not good enough."

"Wait, do you think one of the girls was stealing?"

"Potentially."

"Look," I said. "I had my eyes on the tills all night. No way could one of the waitresses have stolen two hundred bucks, plus I know them. I seriously doubt any of them did it. A few hundred dollars compared to ten grand. I think you can just put that down to simple little mistakes made across the night. As I said, we were *super* busy, so it shouldn't be surprising."

"Someone has to account for the missing money."

"Well, maybe you would know who you think stole it if you'd left the office at any point tonight and actually *helped* us."

I didn't mean for those words to come out as strongly as they did. I was tired, overworked, and stressed, and so I lashed out.

But, seeing Trevor's face when I finished speaking, I knew I'd made a mistake. I'd gone too far.

"How dare you insinuate something like that, Abby," he said, his volume rising. "You're trying to cover up something here. Maybe it was you who stole the money."

"What the hell are you talking about?"

"You're so keen to write it off. Maybe it was you."

"As I told you, Trevor, it was a busy day. There are a million ways that money could've disappeared."

"Maybe you stole the money."

"Are you actually accusing me of this, Trevor?"

"Maybe I am. It's a sackable offense, Abby."

I was gob smacked. I couldn't believe what I was hearing. "What?"

"My question is," Trevor continued, his frown transitioning into a slight smile. "What are you going to do about it?"

"Excuse me?"

"What are you going to do about the accusation? I could get you fired just like *that*."

Trevor raised his hand and snapped his finger next to my face just to emphasize how much power he had there.

I suddenly caught onto the realization of where he was going with this.

The man was trying to blackmail me. Get me to do something in return for not firing me. He'd found something – the disappearance of a few hundred dollars from the tills – and was planning on blaming it on me.

Unless I did something for him.

But what will it be?

"What can I do about it?" I asked, my voice feeling small and tense. I was afraid of what he was going to say. What he was going to suggest.

"How about a drink?" my manager asked, winking at

me. "How about I buy you a drink? A proper one instead of this." He nodded at the bottle I gripped tightly in my hands.

"Yeah?"

This was it. He wanted to take me on a date.

And I couldn't say no.

I couldn't risk being fired.

Trevor had all the power, and he knew it. We both knew that his accusations would work on the owner of O'Malley's, no matter how baseless they were. I'd have no chance. He could get me fired in a finger snap if he wanted to, and we both knew it.

He really was blackmailing me.

"I know that tomorrow's your day off, right?"

I was stunned.

"Yeah."

"How about tomorrow night, then? Does that work for you?"

* * *

I UNLOCKED the front door of my apartment building and stepped inside. I started climbing the stairs, quiet because of how late at night it was. I didn't want to disturb my neighbors.

My mind was still racing from what had just happened at the bar. How Trevor had blackmailed me into a date, and how I did absolutely nothing to stop him. I knew I couldn't have done anything.

The past four years I'd thought I was strong, I thought I'd become independent when I moved out of home and escaped my stepdad, but that night at O'Malley's only proved to me of how much I was still just a scared little girl unable to defend herself.

I had no choice. I would just have to go on a date with Trevor. It was either that or get fired.

And I couldn't afford to lose my job.

Not whilst I was still the sole caregiver for Serenity.

My dignity would have to take a backseat for her security. I had to pay for the roof over our head, for the food in our fridge, and for the pills she had to take.

I'd just have to have a drink with Trevor. Grin and bear it. That's all.

One drink.

Hopefully, that would be enough for him.

Inside my apartment building, I reached my level.

And, just like the night earlier, my neighbor's door was ajar. Light spilled out of it into the dark hallway.

Again? At this time of night? I thought my neighbor would've moved out by now. Isn't that what he'd said yesterday?

"Mr. Clarke?" I asked softly, approaching the open doorway. "Mr. Clarke, are you alright?"

It really was just like the night before.

Reaching my neighbor's apartment, I slowly pushed on the door. It opened fully, allowing me to look in.

And what I saw wasn't Mr. Clarke.

There was a young man, his back turned to me. He was standing in the middle of the apartment's living room, next to a pile of cardboard boxes, similar to Mr. Clarke's ones, but different. These were new boxes, freshly delivered. The man was cutting open one with a knife.

This must be the new neighbor.

Even only viewing the back of him, I could clearly see how muscular he was. A straight posture. Thick arms. Broad shoulders. The man was an athlete. On top physical form.

Even with his short hair, I recognized him.

Even though he appeared older, I knew that body anywhere.

And then, as if sensing the door had opened, he turned around to face me. And at that moment, everything was confirmed for me. My instincts were right.

It was him. Standing there in front of me.

My old neighbor.

Miles Hunter.

25

MILES

SHE STOOD there in the doorway, staring at me. And I stared back.

Fuck. Fuck. Fuck.

Her expression was a mixture of surprise and anger. I couldn't blame her for being that way. I would be pretty surprised too if I suddenly saw a ghost from the past I'd thought was long gone, and I would be even more angry if that ghost was an old boyfriend who was standing in the apartment next to your own.

Fuck. Fuck. Fuck.

This was not how this was supposed to play out. Not with me, unaware, half-opening a box of my belongings past midnight midweek. This wasn't what I had planned.

But there she was. *Abby Starr.* In the doorway, her face pale as she gawked at me.

Fuck.

I had to face the reality of the situation.

And it's a pretty crazy one.

I dropped the knife I was using to open the cardboard box and fully turned to her.

Bracing myself for what came next.

This is definitely not how I expected this to go.

"What are you doing here?" Abby eventually asked, her mouth still hanging open.

"It is a..." I began to speak, but she violently cut me straight off.

"Are you robbing the place?"

"*What?*"

How did she get that idea?

Oh, right. The boxes. Me. The knife. The open door. The empty apartment.

Right.

Yeah, it did look like that, didn't it?

"I'm not robbing the place," I said softly, trying not to inflame the obvious rising tension between us. It felt like Abby would lunge at my throat at any moment. "This apartment is mine."

Abby still stood in the doorway, refusing to move, or perhaps she was simply unable to. Perhaps she was rooted to the spot. She must've had a *hell* of a shock seeing me there like that.

And now she thinks I'm robbing the place. Well, nothing could be further from the truth.

"I. Don't. Believe. You."

Her voice had also quieted down. Into something menacing. She pronounced each word with staccato, emphasizing the venom in her voice. The anger she had for me. A scowl had replaced the shocked expression on her face, and now I was *terrified*.

"I can show you the rental agreement if you'd like," I replied, gesturing to a cardboard box behind me. I was telling the truth. I did have the rental agreement somewhere within the pile of boxes.

It was clear my explanation did little to calm Abby down.

"What the *fuck* are you doing here?" she asked again, even more aggressively.

It would've been hilarious to chide her on her use of foul language, but I assumed it wasn't the time for a joke.

"This apartment is mine," I said. "I'm renting it. Legally."

"Bullshit."

"It's true."

"What are you doing here, Miles? Where have you been all this time?"

"It's a long story."

"I bet it is," she barked back sarcastically.

"If you'd just let me talk," I said.

"I can't believe this is happening," Abby whispered, ignoring me.

It's time to come clean and tell her everything.

"Look, I can explain what happened and why I'm here."

"I don't want to hear your explanations," she replied, waving a furious arm at me. "I don't want to hear anything from you. I don't want to see you again, you got that?"

"That'll be hard, seeing as I'm now living next to you."

"You don't seem surprised to see me," she said, her hand gripping the door tighter. "Not nearly as surprised as I am to see you. In fact, you don't seem shocked at all that we're now neighbors."

"What can I say?"

"Was this planned? Did you move here on purpose?"

"It's more complicated than that," I replied.

"Are you following me? Did you stalk me?"

"It's not like that."

"I really can't believe this."

"Well, I'm here now," I replied. "This is my apartment now."

"You left me," she muttered. Her voice was breaking. Her eyes glistened with tears. Gone was her angry expression, and all that was left was that lonely girl I loved on a dark night four years before. "You disappeared."

"I know." My voice was also small. I also felt tears in my eyes.

I hadn't cried for a very long time. Maybe the last time was four years ago. The time I had to leave her.

"You used me, and then you dumped me. That hurts."

"I really can explain."

"Can you, though?" Abby asked, her voice choking up with emotion. "Can you *really* though? Can you explain four years of pain? Four years of a broken heart? I wouldn't think so."

"It's hard, but trust me, I can explain."

"*Trust you*? After everything you did? You're kidding me."

"I'm not."

"Don't you dare think I'm ever going to listen to you, Miles. Not after what hell you've put me through when you disappeared. You were there, and then you were suddenly gone. Do you even comprehend how that made me feel? I waited for you for such a long time, only for you to turn up now in the fucking apartment next to mine? What the actual *hell*, Miles? What even is happening? What the actual fuck are you doing here, out of everywhere in the world you could be?"

"You're asking me questions, but you don't want me to explain myself?"

Abby grunted and turned away from the door, back into the hallway. "It's late. This is going to take me a long time to process. I need to make sure my sister's taken her medication. I'll have to deal with you another day."

"Right."

"Get out of this apartment," she said, walking out of the room. "I never, ever want to see you again. Understood? I don't care if you have a tenancy contract or even the goddamn Declaration of Independence on you. Get the fuck out of this place."

And then she slammed my door close.

I stood there next to all my belongings in cardboard boxes and comprehended what had just happened.

She didn't give me a chance to speak. If she did, then maybe she would get the answers she was looking for.

Because Abby was wrong.

She was wrong about everything.

But I was smart enough to realize she wasn't going to listen to me in person. No. It would take a lot more than that to get her attention.

Her heart had been broken. It was understandable.

She was shocked by me. Angry.

The very last two things I wanted her to feel.

I would have to explain myself to her somehow. Make her understand what had happened.

And that's when I turned to the kitchen table. I knew what I had to do. I sat down, pulled out a pen and a piece of paper, and started writing a letter addressed to my new neighbor.

26

ABBY

I woke up with a roaring headache, in that strange state between asleep and awake. The worst kind of state to wake up in. I was groggy. It was like I hadn't slept at all.

My head was turning because of one man.

It was all because of Miles Hunter.

Slowly, the events of the night before flooded back to me. As I slowly woke, I lay in bed, racked with the memories of last night.

I wanted to be sick.

The ghost from my past had moved in. My old neighbor. The man I had tried to keep locked away in the little black safe under my bed had come back to life and was now living in the apartment just one thin wall away.

Surely, it couldn't be a coincidence that he'd turned up like that again? Surely not.

Out of all the places, out of all the apartment buildings in all the world, he ended up in the room next to mine.

No freaking way that could be just a roll of the dice.

It was a million-to-one chance.

But, still, he was there in the apartment next door.

And I still couldn't believe it. I didn't know what to do.

Yeah, this is worse than waking up with a hangover.

I had seen a ghost, and I didn't know whether to feel angry or shocked.

Or scared.

"There's a letter under the door!"

Serenity.

She must've already been up. I could hear her roaming about in the living room outside my bedroom door. Probably eating sugary cereal, the only thing I could get her to eat as a teenager.

"What?" I called out, trying to rise from my bed. I rubbed my forehead, attempting to erase the headache. It wasn't working.

"Under the door," my sister called out again. "There's a letter."

A letter?

Strange. Mail went to our letter boxes downstairs by the front door, never to our actual apartments.

Groaning, I managed to stand. I needed to get up. Wake up properly. Shake off this funk I was in.

Thanks, Miles Hunter.

I emerged from the bedroom in a ramshackle state. I sensed my sister's eyes take me in, from my messy hair to my sunken face.

Ugh.

I just wanted to roll back into bed like a sloth.

"What's the letter?" I asked.

"I dunno. Let me check."

Serenity energetically launched from the kitchen counter to the front door, picking up the folded piece of paper.

"Pass it here, please," I said before she could start reading. Curious, Serenity handed it to me.

I unfolded it and locked eyes with the first two words.

DEAR NEIGHBOR,

OH, my God.

There were more words underneath it - a whole letter full - but I refused to read it.

My fist curled around the piece of paper, crushing it in my fingers.

What the *hell* was Miles playing at with this little stunt?

Did he know how much it would hurt me?

He knew the letter's symbolism. He knew what emotions posting it under my door would stir in me.

But I had control over what I felt now. I was no longer the desperate teenager needing his protection. I was my own woman now. I dealt with my problems.

And this was a problem that needed to be dealt with straight away.

That's it.

A sleepless night and now this the next morning? I knew I had to put a stop to it all before I went insane.

He was the one who disappeared. *He* was the one who never wrote me a letter during those months after he left when I really needed one. And now he thought he could just turn up out of the blue and just slip one under my door and everything would be okay?

Is he mad?

What did he think would happen when he saw me last night? That I'd rush into his arms when he said some sweet words like how much he missed me or something? Did he think I would easily forget the weeks and years of pain he left etched into my soul by his wordless disappearance?

Did he think he'd win me over that easily?

What the fuck is he doing back here?

With the letter in my hand, I crossed the room to my apartment's door. I swung it open and marched over to Miles' apartment, banging my fist furiously against his door.

My sister watched on from our own doorway, blinking in confusion at my sudden anger. She didn't speak a word. I didn't tell her what I was doing. She didn't understand what was going on at all.

She didn't know who'd just moved in next door.

Well, she was about to find out. A moment after I knocked on his door, Miles casually opened up, as if he was expecting me.

"Hello," he said, speaking cheerfully, as if nothing had happened in four years. As if we were still sitting next to each other in History class.

I lifted the crumpled piece of paper in his face. "What's the meaning of this?"

Miles shrugged nonchalantly. "My explanation," he replied.

I noticed his appearance. Deep red eyes. His short hair tousled. His skin pale. He looked worse than I did after my sleepless night, and that was saying a lot.

And that pissed me off even more.

"Drunk, are you?" I asked, scanning him up and down.

"No. I don't drink," he replied, leaning lazily against his doorframe only inches from my face. "Not anymore. Not for a long time."

"I don't believe you."

"You don't have to, but it's the truth. I don't drink."

"Then why do you look such a... mess?"

"Because I've been up all night. Thinking of you."

"I don't care."

I wanted to hurt him somehow. Show him how much he hurt me all those years ago. I knew it was a terrible thought to consider, but I did.

Does he actually believe saying that he was up all night thinking of me will make me forget four years of pain?

But I could see my words didn't sting him. They washed off him like water on rocks.

"Read it," he said. "Read the letter and then you can shout at me."

"Don't tell me to do anything."

"Read it and then maybe you might understand. Then you'll have every right to get angry at me."

"Screw you," I replied. "Get out of this apartment building. Get out of my life."

I stormed back into my apartment, showing him my back like I did the night before. Childish, I knew, but I was so built up with anger that I wanted to make a scene.

My sister scurried back inside as I came over, slamming our apartment's door behind me.

"Was that who I thought it was?" she asked.

I nodded, trying to calm myself.

"What's he doing next door?"

I threw the crumpled letter into the trash can. "He lives there now," I curtly replied.

She knew the history between our former - now current – neighbor and me. How could she not?

How could she not tell that someone broke her sister's heart? How could she not tell when I cried every night for a month straight in the hostel after he left, waiting for him to return to me? When we escaped from our stepdad's home, I had to tell her what happened between Miles and me.

But I'd kept his letters hidden from her. They were a part of me I kept hidden from the world.

"He lives there? Next door to us?" my sister asked as I collected myself.

"Yep. As of yesterday."

"What's he doing? Why has he moved in? Is it about you?"

I sighed and rubbed at my headache again. "I don't know, and I don't care. I wish he'd just leave and disappear again."

"Is he stalking you? Should we call the police or something?"

"And they'll do what? I don't know. I'm just so, so tired. I'm going back to bed."

I slumped back off into the dark inviting bedroom, leaving my sister pondering over her bowl of cereal.

I didn't want to call the police on him. Miles wasn't doing anything wrong.

I just wanted to never think of him again. It'd taken me four years to finally pick up the pieces of my broken heart and store the memories of him away in that hidden safe.

But, just like that, he was back in my life.

And I just wanted to sleep.

* * *

SERENITY WOKE ME UP. I'd finally managed to drift off when I was startled by her shaking me awake.

"What is it?" I asked breathlessly, worried there was an emergency. That there was a fire or something, or worse - she was sick again.

"You've slept all afternoon," she whispered, now wary of poking the sleeping beast.

Too late for that.

"Really?"

"It's super late."

"It's my day off."

She thrust something into my hands. It was paper. "You should read this letter," my sister said.

Miles' letter.

What?

"You've read it?" I asked.

Serenity ignored me. "You need to read it."

"You shouldn't have read it, Serenity."

"Well, *sorry*, but I did," she replied, evidently not sorry at all. "You should definitely read it."

"I'm not going to."

I scrunched up the piece of paper for a second time and chucked it into the trash can next to my bed. Where I hoped it would stay. I never wanted to hear about it ever again.

"Well, you better get up," my sister said. "It's nearly six."

"Six? No way."

"Yep."

And then I remembered.

"Oh shit," I said, catapulting out of bed in a frenzy. "Oh shit. Oh shit. Oh shit."

"What is it?" Serenity asked, giggling at my panic and the stream of swear words flowing from my mouth.

I turned to her, my eyes wild. I couldn't believe I'd nearly forgotten about it.

"The date with my boss. It's tonight. It's *now*."

27

ABBY

"WHAT DO you think of this place?" Trevor asked me.

I spun my head to look around the bar we were sitting in, following my boss's gaze. I'd never been there before. I'd passed the place a couple of times before as it was situated between my apartment building and a subway station, but I'd never been inside.

It wasn't anything *spectacular*, just your stereotypical bar. Sports played on large TV screens around the room. A bunch of drunk guys sat yelling politics at each other in the corner. A few girls battered their eyelashes at some cocky dudes who entered. Nothing unusual about it at all. Just your average neighborhood bar.

"It's great," I replied, observing Trevor's reaction. I was careful of not upsetting him or of feeling ingenuine.

Just get through this date. Keep the man happy. Keep your job.

Why did he take me to some random average bar and not to some fancy date place downtown? Wouldn't somewhere like that be nicer for a date? I hoped it wasn't just because of how close this bar was to my apartment.

But, deep down, I knew that was probably the reason.

I shifted in my seat and gave him a forced cheerful smile.

Just keep him happy.

"What would you like to drink?" Trevor asked me, standing.

"A beer, thanks."

"Me too," he said. "Don't go anywhere."

He pointed at me. He laughed like he was joking, but the gesture felt like a threat.

I fake-smiled again. "Oh, I won't."

He chuckled to himself and headed to the bar.

I breathed out. It felt like I'd been holding my breath since I'd arrived at the bar, where Trevor messaged me to meet him. After Serenity woke me, I'd been in a whirlwind of panic, making sure I made it to the place on time. I showered and dressed in chaos. No way did I want to be late. Not when my job was on the line.

Not when I was being blackmailed.

Thinking of the situation like that made it sound so dark.

No, it's just your boss asking you out for a drink. That's all.

Asking me out on a date and threatening to fire me if I didn't.

That was etched-in-stone blackmail.

I told myself to shut up and just continue sitting there. To just get through the date. It was merely a harmless drink in a public bar, nothing to freak out about. Have a few drinks with Trevor, laugh at his stupid jokes, pretend to listen to his inane stories, and get through the night.

My boss returned with our drinks.

He chinked my glass.

"To the future," he cheered.

"To the future," I repeated.

"Tell me about where you live," Trevor said, leaning over the table once he sat back down close to me. "Do you live with others or on your own?"

"Actually, I live with my sister..."

I didn't even get to finish my sentence before he interrupted me.

"Well, I live on my own, not with anyone else," he said. I sat back and sealed my lips. Of course, he wanted to talk only about himself. "I find it easier that way. Better. I get to do what I like when I like. Bring home whoever I like, if you get what I mean. I'm a single man making decent money in the city."

He said it in a self-congratulatory way, and I had to find a way to hide my disgust. The *decent* money he was talking about earning was off the backs of the other waitresses at O'Malley's. He earned that money by doing nothing more than just resting with his feet up in the back office, not helping the poor girls relying on tips by serving customers.

Instead of blurting out something I knew I'd regret, I reached for my beer and took a sip.

Trevor continued like that for the next few hours, talking about himself. I don't think I spoke more than a couple of sentences at all. It was like I was merely window dressing. An obedient trophy wife next to him. A silent therapist. He rattled through his life story, recalling events I'd heard him talk about numerous times at work. He was an old record player repeating the same song. He moved onto his political beliefs, half-baked that they were. It seemed like he got most of his ideas from obscure YouTube videos and the rest from cable TV news. A regurgitation of pointless drivel, not the kind of evening I wanted to spend in the company of.

But I had no option but to lean back and listen to the man.

Eventually, I had enough. My eyes flickered to the clock on the wall.

"It's nearly midnight," I said when Trevor was taking a breather midway through a rant of the evils of modern feminism. "I'd better head home. I'm opening the bar in the morning."

"So am I. It's still so early, though," Trevor replied. And then his eyes flashed at the realization of what "going home" might mean. I didn't mean it that way, but I saw him reflecting eagerly on the possibilities. "Let's go, though. I'm getting bored with this place."

Now he was excited about *going home.*

He led me out of the bar. I wrapped my coat around my shoulders and silently prayed I could get back to my apartment easily.

My boss stopped on the sidewalk outside, pulling out his phone. The screen's light illuminated his craggy face. "Let me get us a taxi," he said, scrolling up the car-share app on his phone.

I raised a hand to his. "Oh, it's okay, Trevor," I said softly. "I'm happy to walk home."

"You sure?"

I nodded in the direction of my apartment building, a few blocks down the street. "I don't live too far away. There's no need to call a taxi for me."

The truth was I didn't want to owe him anything and I couldn't afford a taxi anyway, not with how I was saving all my money to afford Serenity's medication.

"Well, I'll walk with you, then."

"There's no need. I'm okay. Don't trouble yourself."

Please don't walk me home, please don't.

But Trevor saw my reluctance as a silent plea for him to act like a white knight.

"Don't you fret about me, Abby," he replied. "I'll gladly walk you home."

He sounded like some pompous Regency gentleman.

But I didn't dare reject him.

"Only if it's okay with you."

Please say no. Please say no.

"I'll walk you home. You never know what can happen. The streets are not safe sometimes."

I wanted to say to him that I traveled an hour into the city every time I went to work and, therefore, I was perfectly capable of walking a few blocks on my own, but I bit my tongue and went along with him. I just constantly repeated to myself how close the end of the date was.

Just get through the next twenty minutes.

The walk back home was awkward. Trevor didn't say much. It seemed like his mind was on other things.

I found out what those things were when we reached my apartment building.

"Thanks for tonight," I said to my boss as I unlocked the front door and stepped into the main lobby.

Instead of leaving, Trevor also took a step inside my apartment building.

"You're not going to say goodbye without a goodnight kiss, are you?" he asked quietly, his eyes gleaming in the faint light of the lobby. His ugly face moved in close to mine.

"A kiss?" I asked hesitantly.

"Oh, yes. A kiss." I felt his arms reach around my waist, pinning me in place. He enveloped me in the middle of the empty lobby of my apartment building, only a few stairs away from my place, with his face right up against my lips. "You don't want to lose your job now, do you?"

Oh, god.

"No," I replied. "I don't want a kiss."

"Yes, you do. Why else would you go on a date with me?" my boss asked, flashing his teeth at me.

He leaned in even further, his lips puckered.

He was really going to do it.

"No, Trevor," I said, pushing against him, but I couldn't escape.

The night had been a mistake. I should've known it would end like this.

"No!"

But he kept moving in closer, and there was nothing I could do.

"Stop."

The voice came from neither of us. It came from the top of the stairs above us.

Both Trevor and I turned to face the source of the command.

My heart sank when I recognized that face.

Miles Hunter.

He stood in the middle of the stairs leading up to my apartment, glaring down at us. I spotted the outline of his scar under the lobby lights.

"Stop," he repeated. His voice dark.

Trevor looked up at him, his brow creased. Of course, he didn't know Miles or what he meant to me. Our shared history.

"What did you say?" Trevor asked Miles.

"Get away from her."

Trevor shook his head, his arms still firmly gripping my waist. "Mind your own business, weirdo," he replied.

"No," Miles commanded strongly. "Back off."

He'd really changed in the last four years. Gone was the skinny bad boy I knew. Now he was pure muscle. His white t-shirt clung taut against his body, revealing the firm outline of his solid pecs and a hint of a six-pack. The man was built like a quarterback.

Much more physically imposing than Trevor, and they both knew it.

And I knew Miles. I knew the expression on his face, the glint in his eyes. He was ready for a fight.

He wouldn't back down.

I stood still, dumbly staring between Miles and Trevor.

I didn't know what to do. I was afraid of what was going to happen between them.

"And who are you?" my boss asked.

"I'm her neighbor, and I'm ready to call the police." From behind his back, Miles produced a phone and held it in the air, allowing both Trevor and I to see he had 911 ready to dial.

Trevor grunted something inaudible. Letting go of me. He was a self-involved creep, but he was smart enough to know when he was outgunned.

"I'll see you at work tomorrow," he said to me under his breath so that Miles couldn't hear.

It sounded like a threat.

And then he was out the door, his dark coat trailing behind him.

"He left in a hurry," Miles said, descending the stairs towards me.

I glared at him and crossed my arms. "I didn't need you. I can handle myself, thank you very much."

"Evidently."

"Look," I said, pointing at Miles accusatorily. "I don't need you to act like some *protector* over me, alright? I never asked for you to come back into my life. I never asked for you to appear out of nowhere and start *living* next door. Being my neighbor doesn't make you responsible for me, you got that?"

"Got it," Miles replied casually as he reached the bottom step.

"Just because you can appear with all your *muscles* doesn't mean I need you to save me, alright?"

"Message received, Abby," Miles said softly. "That man works with you?"

He was so infuriating.

"He's my boss."

Miles raised an eyebrow. "Interesting," he said. "Where do you work?"

"Some cheesy Irish bar downtown called O'Malley's," I replied. "But why do you care?"

I shook my head and brushed past him, up the stairs towards my apartment. I was not prepared to reward Miles with some kind of long conversation in the middle of the lobby. I was going into my apartment. Away from him.

"I really don't want to talk to you," I said as I rushed past him, my head bowed.

I ascended the stairs to the sound of Miles making one last comment.

"I can see that."

28

ABBY

I LOCKED the door behind me and exhaled. So much pent-up frustration and tension were built up inside me, and I had to let it go somehow. My hands shook.

I was not over what just happened out there.

Trevor just tried to kiss me. He had me pinned down.

Trying to forget what had just occurred in the lobby of my apartment building, I staggered into the kitchen, aiming straight for the fridge. I opened it, desperately reaching in and grabbing a half-eaten bar of chocolate lying on the top shelf. I knew the fridge was a weird place to store chocolate, but I liked it cold. I bit into the bar and savored the taste. I liked to eat chocolate when stressed.

And, right then, I was pretty damn stressed.

How the hell am I going to go into work tomorrow after what's happened out there with my boss?

I leaned on the kitchen counter and closed my eyes.

How could I avoid Trevor when I had to work with the man? How would we resolve what occurred tonight? He was going to make my life hell the next day, I just knew it, if he hadn't already fired me by the time I arrived at O'Malley's in the morning.

And I couldn't afford to lose that job.

"Fuck," I whispered out loud to myself in the kitchen. I was caught in a bad place. Either give in to Trevor's demands or lose my only source of income. Work with the man who just tried to forcefully kiss me or end up on the street?

What to do? What to do?

From outside my apartment, I heard the shuffling of feet up the stairs and the clanging of keys as Miles unlocked the door next to mine. My head turned to the wall that separated our two apartments. Just a few inches of wall lay between us. I had the sudden sobering realization of just how close Miles actually was. A few inches of wall. That was all there was.

Why is he back?

That's what I didn't understand. Still.

Why didn't he seem surprised to see me?

He'd grown up a lot physically in four years, but he still hadn't lost that cocky smile of his. He wasn't shocked to see that we were neighbors when I first saw him the night before. His cocky smile was plastered over his face when he saw me standing there in his doorway.

Yep, him moving in next door is more than just a coincidence.

Was he following me? Would I really have to call in the police?

What was he doing there?

Was it all to do with me?

What had he been doing for four years?

Questions sped through my mind as I leaned against the

kitchen counter, biting into my chocolate. Questions about Miles.

And I realized I knew nothing about him.

We had only known each other for a few weeks, four years ago.

He was a stranger. And now he was back in my life.

I was just so confused.

By everything. Miles. Trevor. Work and money.

I felt so alone.

My head spun.

My focus shifted to the bedroom, where Serenity was now sleeping. Where the so-called *explanation* letter from Miles lay crumbled in my trash can next to my bed. Apparently, that held the answers to my questions.

Maybe I could fish it out and read it? Serenity certainly thought I should.

But why should I give him the pleasure of reading his lies?

Why am I even being dropped into this mess?

All I wanted to do was work, provide for my sister, and make sure she had a good future, but *men* like Miles - men like *Trevor* - seemed determined to ruin my life and everything I worked hard for. It wasn't fair, and it wasn't easy, but I knew I had to learn to move above it. Move above them. Sink or swim and all that.

I threw the empty chocolate wrapper into the trash and headed to the bedroom, quietly walking on tiptoes as to not wake up my sister.

Miles thought he could saunter back into my life and I'll just play happy little neighbor?

No.

Screw him and his letters.

He meant nothing to me.

29

ABBY

I COULDN'T HELP NOTICING MILES' door to his apartment was closed when I left home the next morning. I'd been worried the entire time I got ready that he'll want to speak to me about what happened the night before, so I was glad he didn't hear me or tried to talk to me as I left.

I did not want to deal with him.

I didn't care for what he had to say.

I left the apartment building and headed on the subway downtown. All the way to work.

The entire ride in, I was nervous. I couldn't sit still, so I anxiously stood in the middle of the train instead, holding onto the rail tightly as the train made its way across the river into the city, trying hard to stop the uncontrollable shaking from spreading throughout my body.

I was freaking out. About work. About Trevor.

Why am I subjecting myself to this? To him?

Serenity. That was why. I was doing this for her.

I had to be strong for her.

I practically speed-walked the few blocks from the downtown station to O'Malley's in an attempt to loosen myself up before I started my shift. I didn't want anyone to see how tumultuous I was. How much I was unhinged inside.

I entered O'Malley's through the staff entrance at the back and I headed straight into the main bar.

Standing there, in the middle of the bar facing each other, were Trevor and Miles.

My face dropped when I saw them both. The two men were close. Miles was muttering something quiet and dark, his blue eyes trained on Trevor. My boss's shoulders were slumped, his head bowed.

They looked completely mismatched. Miles towered over Trevor, his muscular frame seemingly twice the size. His fist must've been the size of my boss's head.

And they were in deep conversation.

"What's going on?" I asked, completely shocked by the sight I was greeted with as I entered work. I dropped my bag and shook my head. The two men standing in the middle of the bar ignored me. Miles continued whispering something to Trevor. Something I couldn't hear. "Hello?"

What the hell is going on? What are the two guys doing?

Miles looked up at me when I spoke for a second time, his face completely blank. He turned back to my boss as if I didn't exist.

"You got it?" he asked Trevor sternly.

Got what?

"Yep," replied my boss. His response was quiet and subdued. He was never like that.

My neighbor's making him like that.

"Good."

Glancing back up at me for one quick look, Miles

turned and left the bar out the front door. I couldn't decipher what his expressionless face meant.

I stood there, still absolutely confused by what had just happened, trying to piece together what I just saw. Miles was warning Trevor about something, maybe even threatening him. The looks my neighbor was giving my boss were ones I'd only seen in gangster films.

Something serious had happened between them, that much I could tell.

And I'm going to get to the bottom of it. I bet it has something to do with me.

"What was that about?" I asked my boss once Miles had left.

Trevor just shrugged, avoiding my gaze. He kept his head bowed, looking at the ground and shuffling his feet. That was so unlike him. Where had the arrogant Trevor I'd known gone?

I didn't like this. Not one bit.

"I need to say something," my boss said, his voice tiny. "About last night..."

"We don't need to talk about it," I replied, trying to avoid any awkwardness.

"I'm sorry for what I did. What I tried to do. It was... *improper* of me."

What?

I had never heard the man admit he was in the wrong, let alone an actual full-blown apology.

What had Miles said to him?

I really wasn't liking what this was about.

"Is this because of what Miles said?" I asked. "Is this because of whatever he told you just then?"

Trevor didn't reply. He just hung his head in shame.

Something was wrong.

Something was *very* wrong.

"Right," I seethed, storming out the bar the same door Miles had left from. I searched the streets for him.

I didn't care about my boss.

I was going to find out what the *fuck* was going on.

I found Miles a block away, heading towards the subway station. I recognized his confident stride instantly.

And I chased up to him. I tapped him on the shoulder aggressively.

"Hey," I said, pissed off. "I don't need your help, Miles."

He stopped and faced me. His blank expression still unreadable. "Sure, you did."

God. He enraged me.

"What did you say to Trevor?"

His face didn't change.

"Not much."

"Come on, he's different because of you. He's not himself this morning. I'm not an idiot; it was clearly something that's rattled him, something you did. What did you say to him? Because he literally just apologized to me back there, and that man never ever apologizes for anything."

Miles clenched his jaw. I saw the muscles stiffen under his perfectly tanned skin.

"You shouldn't get any trouble from him anymore. Let me know if there is."

He was being curt. Mysterious.

Incredibly annoying.

"I'm not letting you know anything," I replied. "Why shouldn't I get trouble from him? What did you say to him, Miles? Stop being so damn aloof."

I sensed his eyes trailing over me. I saw what was in them.

Desire

It was burning within them, the blue of his eyes bright.

Now I know what he's thinking.

204

I took a step back.

So, he wanted me, but why?

Why after all these years? Why didn't he stay four years ago when we had the chance to be together? What made him disappear if he still wanted me now?

"Look, I was in the Army," he said. "I know how to scare someone. Let's leave it at that."

The Army?

Was that what he was doing all this time?

It would explain his muscles, that's for sure, and why he'd changed so much physically.

But I didn't show any concern for him or his *Army* explanation. That's not how things worked. I wouldn't excuse him just because he wore a uniform.

"You threatened my boss. Is that what you're saying?"

"I was looking out for you."

Screw that.

"Well, I don't need it. Like I said last night, I don't need your *protection*."

"Seems like you did. That man was troubling you. Now he's been stopped. I was looking out for you, simple. If it wasn't for me, then he would be hurting you."

Hurting me?

"You were the one who disappeared, remember? So, don't lie, you were never and have never looked out for me. *You* hurt me."

"I did what I had to do four years ago," Miles said, casting a downward glance to the ground. "However much I might want to relive it and do things differently, I can't. But you can't change the past, right?"

Yeah, I hope he feels guilty for what he did. He should be.

"No, you can't change the past, Miles, but you can apologize for it," I replied.

A smile crept over his face.

"Read the letter," he said. "Everything's there."

Oh.

That stupid fucking letter.

"Well, stick your letter up your ass," I replied. I had enough of him. His cocky smirk had returned, and I couldn't stand it.

I spun around and stormed back towards the bar.

I had enough of his *explanations*.

I didn't care what he'd been doing for four years. I didn't care if he was in the Army or even if he was freaking James Bond. The guy had left me, and now he decided that my life was worth saving? No way. He wanted to butt in on my problems now? Play the savior card?

I headed back to O'Malley's, and I didn't turn around to check back on him. In my mind, he really could just go and fuck off.

30

ABBY

FUCK IT.

I was going to read it. It had been bothering me all day since I chased him down the street downtown in the morning. It had been on my mind all through my shift at work. When Trevor had acted all docile and meek towards me.

It had been all I was thinking about all day, and now I just had to read it.

Curiosity was killing me.

Miles had definitely said something incredibly threatening to my boss. There was no way he was acting that well-behaved way if he hadn't been scared shitless by Miles. It was amazing, seeing how much Trevor had changed in the blink of an eye, in one single quiet conversation with my neighbor.

Miles had got to him somehow.

And it made me even more curious.

Yep. Fuck it.

I had to read the letter.

I pulled myself off the couch and turned off the TV. I was pretty sure Serenity would be sleeping in the other room. I had sent her to bed an hour earlier, making sure she had enough shut-eye for school the next day, whilst I sat in the living room of my apartment thinking endlessly about that letter in the trash can. The letter I had never wanted to read, but now I was itching for it.

Miles' explanation.

That's what it was.

Well, hopefully, it can explain why he ghosted on me for years. That would definitely take a lot of explaining to do.

Yep. Fuck it.

I quietly opened the door to the bedroom Serenity and I shared. I spotted her body under her bedsheets, sleeping. I didn't want to disturb her, so I only opened the door a crack, slowly leaned over, and fished the crumpled letter from the trash.

She didn't stir.

Good.

Silently closing the bedroom door, I resumed my spot on the couch and unfolded the letter, smoothing it out so I could see it better.

I took a deep breath.

And then I started reading.

DEAR NEIGHBOR,

I don't know how to start this letter, I really don't. This is going to be really hard to write.

No, I'm lying...

This letter is practically impossible to write.

This letter is going to be the hardest thing I've ever tried to put down into words.

How do you begin to write down years of pain?

I certainly don't know how.

I have been sitting here at my stupid desk for literally an hour just trying to think of all the things I could say to you - all the explanations I could write on this piece of paper - but I have come up with absolutely nothing. Zilch. The stuff I've written down so far? I've simply thrown them in the trash. There's literally a pile of torn-up bits of paper right next to me right now. I've even bitten a pen because of how frustrated I've been, and now there's blue ink everywhere.

I don't know why I wrote that. It feels like something you would find funny. Something you could laugh at me about.

I wish I could make you laugh again. That's when I find you the most attractive. When your lips curl up and you snort in that super embarrassing way you do. I wish I could see that again. I wish I could hear you laugh again.

There's a lot I want to say to you, but every time I try to write it down there just simply aren't enough words in the English language to accurately describe what I'm thinking.

Believe me, this letter really is really, really impossible to write.

So. Fuck it. I'm just going to ramble on like this, and I'm just going to let all the words out in no order.

Here goes.

I know you didn't expect to see me last night. I certainly didn't. When I pictured you seeing me again, it was not in that way, with me standing there with the door open like that.

I thought - somehow in my thick brain – that I would make it easy for you in some way, but clearly, I was wrong. Last night definitely did not go as I intended at all.

I know you want answers. It is completely fair that you do. I totally would if I was in your position. And, seeing as to how you reacted last night, I know there's a lot for me to explain. I know I'm going to have to do a lot of writing here to even come close to getting you to understand what's happened in the time since we've last seen each other.

There is a lot to tell you.

I know you don't trust me, and I don't expect you to, but what you're going to read written down here is the whole truth. Everything ripped from my soul.

My truth.

My explanation.

And maybe it's enough. Maybe it can help you. Maybe it can explain at least something.

There's never been anyone else. There has always only been you.

Let me confess...

AND WHAT FOLLOWED WAS Miles letting his heart out. Everything he had done in the last few years.

Everything.

From the very first words of that letter, I started to cry, and I didn't stop until I finished the final word.

31

TWO MONTHS EARLIER

MILES

THE SEATS of the car were both familiar and foreign to me. Riding in it again was weird after all this time. I vividly remembered the touch of the leather covers and the clean smell of the car. I'd ridden in the back of the vehicle all through my teenage life, but it had been four years since I had last sat inside it.

A lot had happened in four years.

Driving through the town brought back the same feelings. The roads and houses were the same. We passed by the high school. Even though I only attended there for a few weeks, there were still a lot of memories residing in that old brick building.

Memories of Abby Starr.

I sighed and leaned back in the car seat, closing my eyes

and trying to blank my mind as we drove past the high school. I was frustrated with myself. We'd only been driving in the town for a few minutes and already memories of that girl were flashing in my mind. Must've been a record or something.

My parents had picked me up at the airport. I just had a few bags with me when I landed. In them was my entire life for the past four years. Everything I owned.

"We're nearly home now, son." Dad's eyes stared at me through the rearview mirror once we passed the school. I matched his stern gaze and then quickly looked away, back out the window at the town flickering past.

"Yeah," I replied. "Home."

Dad pulled us in front of the house. More memories flooded back to me as I stepped out of the car. I looked next door. At Abby's house.

Was she there?

What had happened to her?

Why had she never received my letters?

I followed my parents through the front door. My mom patted me on the arm.

"Four years of active duty, and now you're home," she said softly.

I nodded and headed for my old bedroom. I needed to be on my own.

There was a lot to take in, and I was not prepared to deal with it.

In some sick way, it was funny. I was a soldier. I knew how to prepare for any situation. I knew how to respond to any physical conflict. Strip a gun and all that. I knew how to be – *to live* - in a war zone. I knew how to keep my cool under any warlike situation, but coming back home and standing in my old house's hallways destroyed me inside and out.

This was something I couldn't prepare for. Something I couldn't deal with.

Years in a combat zone and yet I couldn't face my own home.

I closed my bedroom door behind me and dumped my bags on the freshly made bed. I walked over to the window and peered outside across the yard at Abby's house.

It had been years since I last step foot in that room.

A lot had changed.

Outside Abby's house was a young boy playing with a soccer ball, bouncing it off the wall. Kicking it with his foot. I watched him for a moment, curious as to why he might be there. Abby never mentioned a brother. Maybe he was a family friend?

And then the front door of the house opened. Out came a middle-aged man. He gestured to the kid. "Come inside, Jake. Dinner's ready."

And then I got it.

It was a different family living in that house. It wasn't where Abby lived anymore.

She might not have been living there for years.

I sat down in my chair and gripped the armrests.

My parents never told me that. They never said Abby had moved.

They lied to me.

I knew then that the reality I had imagined for four years, the reality that Abby didn't even want to talk to me, had been a complete *lie*. Made up in my head. I thought she didn't want to see me after the night I beat up her stepdad. That she purposely didn't reply to my letters.

But that was all false.

It had never been real.

Dad forced me to enlist the day after I beat up Abby's stepdad. He saw what had happened outside in the dark.

He saw my behavior and thought enough was enough. I had crossed the final line. He took me to the recruitment office the very next day and, with his contacts in the Army, sped along my application process.

I never got to see Abby.

I never got to say goodbye.

I never got to tell her that I was going into the Army.

So, I sent her letters. To explain what was happening. Where I was. But I never got a reply from her.

I thought that was it. That she no longer cared for me.

And now, sitting in my old bedroom looking out at a new family opposite, I knew I had been wrong.

All those years in the Army.

That time our Humvee was attacked. When it all exploded around us. When I stripped all the gear off my friend and carried him back to base, I had been wrong about Abby.

I carried Curtis for miles that day, in the heat and the sand. Away from the bullets. Away from the explosions and the bodies and the pain. All the way back to base, I carried him in my arms.

I wrote letters about it all to Abby, thinking she no longer gave a fuck. I unloaded all my emotions in those letters.

And now I knew she never even got the chance to read them.

There was a knock on my bedroom door. It was my mom calling to say that dinner was ready.

I quietly left my room and sat down at the dinner table. Dad watched me with his dark little eyes as I took my place opposite him.

"So, what are your plans now that you're back? What's your future going to be?" he asked me once our plates were full.

I never wanted to sit around that dinner table again. And I especially didn't want to be quizzed about my future from my father.

"I don't know," I replied quietly.

"Well, you need to give it some thought. You can't stay holed up in your bedroom like you were as a teenager, you know."

"I know."

"You've got to make something of your life."

I took in a deep breath. "I never got the chance to reject being enlisted," I said under my breath.

"What?"

But my dad had heard me. He heard what I said.

"I never got the chance to reject being enlisted," I repeated, finding my voice.

"Say that again." Dad was seething.

And I was happy to oblige him.

"I never wanted to serve," I said. "You forced me to, remember? You took away years off my life, and for what? To see my friends get blown up?"

"You were a deadbeat," Dad replied. "You had to have some discipline kicked into you."

I continued over him. I didn't care what he had to say anymore. I needed to get this out. "My best friend, Curtis, nearly died. I had to carry him back to base. We bled blood together out there in the sand. We bled together in a foreign country I can't even place on a map, and it was all because of you, Dad. You sent your son out there to die, and for what? For you to feel like you have some measure of control in your tiny world?"

The words came flowing out of my mouth, unplanned.

Dad just sat there, taking it all in. His upper lip quivering.

"What did you say?"

"You understand perfectly," I replied. "You sent me out there. I wish I never let you."

"Don't disrespect the military," he barked back.

"I'm not disrespecting anyone I served with," I said, slamming my fist on the table. "I'm disrespecting *you*. How dare you thought you could control my life? How dare you force me to enlist."

"I will not hear you talk about me in that way under my roof."

"Fine," I said, standing. "You don't have to hear me talk ever again."

"Where are you going?"

Dad's face went red. But I didn't care.

I marched straight back to my bedroom. My father called after me as I left the room, but I didn't listen to him.

I would never have to listen to him again for the rest of my life.

I would never have to see him again.

I had said what I needed to say.

I locked my bedroom door behind me, picked up my bags, opened my window, and climbed out into the fresh afternoon air. Freedom.

That was it.

Forever.

Escaping that house was the easiest decision I'd ever made in my life.

I crossed the yard and stood outside Abby's old home. I rang the doorbell and waited silently until the front door opened, revealing the dad I'd seen earlier.

"May I help you?" he asked. He seemed surprised to see someone standing on his doorstep. With my buzz cut and bulging muscles, carrying a few big bags, I knew I must've looked an intimidating sight.

"Hi," I replied. "Sorry to bother you. I'm Miles. I used to live next door. I'm looking for someone."

"Yes?"

"Abby. She used to live here. Do you know where she lives now?"

The man narrowed his eyes. "I don't remember an Abby."

"Her last name was Starr."

"Well, yes. The Starr woman was the person who I bought this place off," the dad replied. "But there wasn't an Abby Starr. I certainly don't remember one."

"You sure? She's my age. She had a younger sister."

"There were only two people who I bought this house off," the dad replied. "Both were much older. There were no younger women at all, not that I can recall. I bought this place three years ago. It's been some time, so I may not remember it correctly."

"Okay. Thank you for your help," I replied.

Damn.

I was going to have to find her another way.

Taking one last glance at my family's house, I started heading in the opposite direction. Towards town. Towards the bus stop. I was planning on getting out of there forever.

As I walked, I pulled out my phone and dialed a friend I knew from the Army. A tech whizz. A guy who once boasted to me that he could locate anyone who owned a computer.

I didn't care how legal his skills were, right then I needed them.

"Hi, Daniel," I said when he answered. "It's me. I want you to find someone."

32

PRESENT DAY

ABBY

I FINISHED MILES' letter and sunk back into the couch. Completely devastated.

He just told me everything. Why he disappeared. Everything that had happened to him in the last four years.

Him being enlisted. Him trying to write to me. His time overseas in the military. Fighting in the sand and in the sun. The time his Humvee was attacked, and how he saved his friend's life by carrying him all the way back to base for medical treatment.

It was all there, written down as words on a page. His entire life from the minute we were forcibly separated four years ago, right up until the present day.

And he wrote of his return home. Him finding out I had moved. How he had never realized that until it was too late. How he tracked me down across the country by using some tech friend of his from the Army. How he purposely rented the apartment next door for one purpose.

He wanted to explain himself to me.

He was planning on renting somewhere nearby, but when next door became available, he snatched it up quickly. He rented that place knowing how difficult I would take his return. But no matter, he wanted to be close to me.

He wanted to see me again.

He wanted to explain everything.

And he did, through this letter. It was all there in black and white. A few thousand words on a page.

I leaned back into the couch and dropped the letter from my hands. My eyes stung. My face was red from crying. The paper in my hands was soggy with my tears.

There was a lot to process. Four years of it, in fact.

But I knew one thing: I had got Miles completely and utterly wrong.

He didn't disappear on me, not on purpose anyway. He didn't ghost me deliberately. He *tried* to stay in touch. We were forced apart.

In a complete reversal, he had thought *I* was the one who wasn't there for him, that *I* was the one who ghosted him.

It all made sense now.

Why he'd moved in next door. Why he came back for me.

He still loved me. He'd never stopped loving me.

And, deep down, I knew I still loved him.

I dragged myself off the couch and headed for the kitchen counter. I fished around for a notepad and a pen, and I started to write.

* * *

MILES OPENED the door to me, kneeling down in front of it.

I froze.

"What are you doing?" he asked. The letter I'd just written was in my hand. I had thought I'd be sneaky and post it under his door, just like he did to mine the other day. It was the middle of the night after all, so I thought he would be asleep and that I'd get away with posting the letter like that.

But Miles must've heard me shuffling about. He opened his apartment door and found me in the stupid position of crouching down, halfway through sliding the letter between the gap.

I laughed nervously and stood back up when he asked me what I was doing, revealing the letter in my hand. "I thought I'll give you a letter."

"I heard something and went to check. I didn't think it would be you."

I flicked my hair back. "Well, it was me. Being a total clumsy idiot in the middle of the night. Sorry to disturb."

Miles' eyes darted to the letter in my hand. "Is that for me?" he asked.

I sighed. "Yep."

"You were going to give it to me?"

"Yep."

"Let me have a look."

I pulled the letter away from his grasp. "No."

"Why not?"

"It feels weird now."

"Why?"

"I don't want you to read it in front of me."

"I won't," he promised. "I'll wait till you go."

I hoped so.

"Alright," I said, handing over the letter. Miles took it in one hand and looked down at it. "It's pretty embarrassing."

"Why do you say that?" he asked.

"Because of what's in it."

"And what's in it?"

I scratched at my arm, fidgeting, and glanced at the floor. "I just read your letter," I replied.

Can he see the tears in my eyes? How red my cheeks are?

He must've.

"And?"

"Yep."

There were no words to accurately describe what I was feeling.

"Yeah?"

"There's a lot to take it," I replied. "A lot to think about."

"I can imagine."

"I never thought..."

But Miles had raised a hand. "It's fine," he said calmly. "It's okay. I understand."

He does?

That was more than enough. He understood. He got the whirlwind of emotions I was feeling. Staring at his bright blue eyes, I knew he could see right through me. He got me.

I smiled. "Goodnight, Miles."

He smiled back. "Goodnight, Abby."

I watched him close the door.

He had my letter. He was going to read it.

I unlocked the door back into my apartment and breathed a sigh of relief.

Miles understood me.

My head was a tumble of thoughts and feelings as I stood alone in the hallway between our two apartments. I couldn't think straight.

But it seemed like everything was good.

And now I needed to sleep.

I locked my door behind me, stepped through my apartment, and opened the bedroom door.

And what I saw made me gasp.

On the floor was Serenity. Her body was shaking uncontrollably. Her eyes were closed.

I knew instantly what was happening. I'd seen it before, four years before.

She was having an attack.

33

MILES

THE FIRST THING I heard from next door was a cry, and then a scream. It sounded urgent. Terrifying.

And it was coming from Abby's apartment.

I sprinted out of my living room and into the hallway. I stood outside Abby's place and listened against her door. There was another cry from inside.

Something's wrong.

I just knew it.

"Abby?" I called through her shut door. "Abby?"

There was no answer.

Something was definitely wrong, but I was stuck outside.

Abby needed help.

I looked around desperately, trying to think of how to get inside her apartment. What if she was in trouble? What if she was unconscious?

She might need me, and I could do nothing standing outside her door.

"Abby?" I yelled her name a few more times. But still. No answer.

Right. That's it.

There was only one thing left for me to do. It was an emergency.

I hope she can forgive me for this.

With all my force, I kicked Abby's door, right where her lock was. It was something I had learned in the Army. The best way to break down a door.

And this time, it worked perfectly.

The door smashed off its hinges, blowing down into her living room. I stormed in, ready for whatever sight greeted me.

I spotted Abby crouching down in her bedroom with a teenage girl - I assumed to be her sister - cradled in her arms. Abby's sister was clearly having some kind of seizure. Her body was rocking, and her face was spasming. It was a horrible thing to see.

Abby turned to me, her face stricken with panic, and uttered one single sad word.

"Help."

I pulled out my phone from my back pocket. "I'll call an ambulance," I said, dialing in 911.

"No," Abby replied, trying to calm her sister by stroking her face. "It'll take too long."

"What do you want me to do?"

Abby didn't pause. "We have to go to the hospital now."

I bit my lip and spun around. "Okay. Should we get a taxi?"

Abby just nodded. She was in shock. So was I. But I knew we had to move fast. This was really serious.

I rushed into her bedroom and leaned over Abby, picking her sister up in my arms.

It's the only thing I can do.

Without hesitation, Abby led me out of the apartment and down the stairs. We went through the lobby and out the front door. We stood on the sidewalk together outside the apartment building. It was dark. Abby. Me. And her sister draped in my arms, standing on the sidewalk in the middle of the night.

This is really happening.

I looked down at Serenity's face as I cradled her in my arms. She was still in the midst of the seizure. I held her carefully, so as to not disturb her. She was light. Skinny. Much easier to carry than my friend Curtis when we were attacked.

In front of us, Abby was frantically flipping her head up and down the street, searching. It was very late at night. There was no traffic. No cars.

No taxis.

"There aren't any," she whispered. Her eyes were white. She was freaking out. She needed my help.

There's one thing I can do.

"I can take her," I said.

"What?"

"I can take her to the hospital."

"With what? You don't have a car."

I glanced down at Serenity in my arms and Abby instantly knew what I was thinking.

"No."

"It's the only way," I replied. "It's the fastest way."

"I... don't know."

"Can you think of any other option?" That stumped her. She knew what I was suggesting was risky, but she also knew it was the best chance we had of getting Serenity to the hospital in time to be treated. "Every moment is against us right now, and this is the best plan I can think of. I have to try."

She thought about it for a moment. A few precious seconds wasted. She nodded. "Okay."

"Follow behind me," I commanded. "I'll keep her safe. I promise."

Abby was crying. She was putting all her trust in me.

But this was the right thing to do. The only thing to do.

I hope I'm right.

I faced down the street in the direction of the hospital, only a dozen or so blocks away. I'd been past it before. I knew where it was.

Yeah, I can make it.

I had to make it.

I had to keep Serenity safe.

With Abby behind me and with her sister in my arms, I started to run.

And I didn't stop until I reached the hospital.

34

ABBY

Miles rose to his feet.

"You want a coffee?" he asked me.

I nodded. "Yes, please."

"Right. I'll be a minute."

I watched him make his way down to the end of our row of seats in the hospital waiting room. He squeezed past other sitting patients and headed towards the coffee shop at the far side of the waiting area. He turned back around, winking at me. I smiled weakly in return.

We'd been sitting in the emergency department at the hospital for nearly two hours by that point, and I was exhausted. The minutes had gone by slowly. The hours felt like forever.

And all I wanted to do was find out if my sister was okay.

My stomach was in knots, but there was nothing I could do. I just had to sit there under the harsh fluorescent lights of the waiting room and patiently bide my time until the doctor reappeared with the results of the medical tests on my sister.

I'd followed Miles all the way to the hospital. He ran there with Serenity in his arms. It was an amazing sight to see, this tall, muscular man carrying my sister nearly a dozen blocks to the tall white building. He didn't break a sweat. Four years in the military had clearly toughened him up.

Thank God for Miles. Without him, I didn't think we would make it.

We definitely wouldn't have made it.

And now I had to wait.

And it was killing me.

Miles returned from the coffee shop with two steaming cups in his hands. He blew on them and gave one to me.

"Thanks," I said as he settled in the plastic seat next to mine. I still hadn't wrapped my head around why he was there and the events of the evening that led to him getting me coffee in a hospital in the middle of the night. But he was a welcome presence.

And I needed a coffee.

It was good to have someone beside me during the whole ordeal. I would've gone mad if I had to wait there on my own.

I sighed and leaned towards him, resting my head on his shoulder and cupping the hot beverage between my hands.

Miles didn't react to me cuddling up beside him. He took a sip of his coffee.

"Well, that's disgusting," he said, making a stupid gargling noise with his mouth. I couldn't help but laugh. I had built up so much stress with nowhere for it to go. His silly little comment just made me unleash an uncontrollable laugh. I needed it. "What's so funny?"

"You. Drinking the coffee."

"Don't laugh at me."

He was being sarcastic. Funny.

"I wasn't laughing at you."

"It really is terrible coffee. Don't drink it, Abby. It's a potentially hazardous material. They should put a radioactive label on the stuff."

"Okay, I won't."

We both went quiet. Miles placed the coffee on the armrest next to him. He reached over with his hand and started stroking my hair as my head rested on his shoulder. A warm feeling started deep within my stomach, and it wasn't coming from the coffee.

"Will everything be okay?" I asked him softly, barely moving my lips to speak.

"It will," he replied slowly, but we both knew he was stabbing in the dark with that hope. We both didn't know how the night was going to end. But it was good for him to say that. It calmed me down.

I watched as a doctor emerged from the doors opposite and checked something over with the receptionist before he called out into the waiting area.

"Abby Starr?"

I raised my arm and lifted my head from Miles' shoulder. "That's me!"

The doctor beckoned me over. Miles followed behind me.

"It's good news," the doctor quietly said to me when I reached him. "Your sister's going to be okay. She's going to have to stay here overnight, but she's okay."

My heart dropped. A sense of relief washed over me like a tidal wave.

"Is she awake?" I asked.

"Yes. You can see her if you like."

"Please."

The doctor led Miles and me deeper into the hospital. I reached out for Miles' hand and he took it. We went down long white corridors until we arrived at Serenity's room.

She was lying in bed. A whole host of medical equipment around her. Signals and bleeps from different machines were monitoring her body. Her eyes were open, and she smiled at us as we entered.

"Serenity," I said as I rushed to her side, hugging her. Her body felt small and weak under mine, but she still managed to wrap her arms around me. It was good to feel her.

"Hey, sis," she said, her voice weak and raspy.

"You gave me a crazy scare," I said, and she smiled again.

"Sorry about that."

"You have nothing to be sorry for. I'm just happy you're awake."

"I think I have Miles to thank for that," she said, nodding at our neighbor standing awkwardly by the door. Miles took a step into the room.

"Hi, Serenity," he said.

"Thank you, Miles. For what you did."

"It was nothing."

"It was everything," my sister replied, and Miles started blushing. His manly cheeks went red.

"He carried you the whole way," I said.

"I know. It's crazy. You're a strong guy, Miles."

He shrugged. "I eat all my vegetables."

My sister turned to me, grabbing my hand tight. "The doctors spoke to me. I'm going to be here all night, Abby," she said. "You should go home."

"I won't leave you, Serenity."

"I'm fine here. I need to sleep. There's no point if you're hovering over me all night."

"No. I can stay here. It's no problem at all."

Miles crouched down next to me. "Your sister's right," he whispered. "You need to go home and sleep, Abby. You're exhausted. Serenity's safe now."

"I'm okay here," my sister said. But that was not enough for me. I wanted to stay. I wanted to be close to her. For some reason, I felt responsible for her seizure.

It had all gone wrong. Because of me.

"I should've been looking after you better," I said, taking hold of her arm with both my hands. Tears welled in my eyes.

"You have. You're the best sister, Abby. What more could you do?"

"I could've done more," I replied. "This was my fault."

In bed, my sister shook her head at me.

"This was no one's fault," Serenity said. "No one's, and especially not yours."

"You're my responsibility. I shouldn't have let this happen. I'm your big sister."

"I'm fine, Abby," Serenity replied calmly. "You've been the best sister. The very best. And now you should go home. I'm okay spending one night here on my own."

I struggled to hold the tears back. I felt Miles' arms blanket around me, a warm cushion. Serenity glanced over to our neighbor.

"Take her home, Miles."

35

MILES

It was hard getting Abby to leave the hospital. She wanted to stay, to be close to her sister. She refused to leave the waiting room, so much so that I had to gently coax her outside with reassurances that Serenity would be fine. That she was in a hospital. That she was in the best place for her to be.

Her sister was right. Abby needed sleep. She looked spent.

So do I.

"You're a good person," I told her as we left Serenity's hospital room. "But you need to go home and rest."

"Can we walk back?" she asked me before I could order a taxi. "I'll like to get some fresh air."

"Sure."

It sounded like a good idea.

We didn't speak much on our walk back to the apartment building. Abby marched with her arms crossed. I enjoyed the opportunity to gently stroll through the night, though. It was nice to be calm and still. The city was quiet around us. Everyone else was sleeping.

It was not until the final block when Abby opened her mouth to speak.

"It's strange taking the same route back from the hospital we just ran on," she said.

"Yeah. I know what you mean," I replied.

We turned the corner. We could see our apartment building in the distance.

"Thank you again for tonight," she said. "For everything. For carrying Serenity all that way."

"So, is this a roundabout way of saying you don't exactly hate me one hundred percent?"

"Don't get too cocky," Abby replied. "I'm still to make up my mind on you."

"On what, exactly?"

"On how much you were lying in that letter."

"Every word of it is true."

"Hmm. We'll see."

"I promise you, everything in that letter is true," I repeated. "I really did think you never sent me a letter for all those years. I never thought that maybe you weren't even receiving the ones I sent. When I came back home and found out I was wrong, I had to use my Army guys to track you across the country like a stalker."

"But why?" she asked. "Why did you move in next door?"

"I had to make sure."

"Make sure of what?"

"That you still liked me."

"I never did stop liking you," Abby replied.

My body went tense and my walking slowed.

That was what I was waiting to hear.

I just never thought I would.

We entered the apartment building, ascending the stairs together. We stopped outside our places, unable to say good-night to each other. Unable to? Or didn't want to?

I wasn't sure.

Abby pointed at her doorway and at the door - the one I had smashed – lying on the ground. "I actually can't believe you did that," she said.

I laughed. "Me too."

Abby covered her mouth, trying to hide a fit of giggles.

"Are you okay staying there whilst the door's broken down?" I asked.

"I dunno," she replied. "Maybe you should stay over. You need to help me look after my stuff now that you broke my door down."

"Really?"

She took a step towards me. "Yep. Anyone could come in."

"You're inviting me to stay over?"

Abby rolled her eyes. "Come here," she said as she grabbed hold of me and brought her lips to mine. I didn't resist.

Making out with her was even better than when we were teenagers. We'd grown into our bodies since then. We were more mature. We both knew what we wanted. I tilted her chin and leaned in closer, wrapping my arms around her. Taking her in. Her fingers sunk into my shoulders as we made out.

She pulled me away from the hallway and the stairs towards her apartment. We stepped over the remains of the broken door, still holding tight on to each other. Our lips still connected.

My body was ready for her. I felt the blood pulse straight to my groin. My cock was hard as Abby pulled me straight into her bedroom and shut the door after us.

"You want this?" I asked.

She didn't need to answer. Her lips parted, and she gasped. Her hands traveled across my body, across my muscles.

She was so eager, so keen. I grabbed hold of her and enticed her to the bed. She fell down upon it, pulling herself back up to grab at my jeans. She tore them down and dug her hand inside my underwear, clutching my erect cock.

The way she looked at me, with her lust burning bright behind her eyes, drove me mad. I just had to have her. I desired her so much that my body felt a raging furnace. I'd never been so hard, so ready to fuck.

"I want to taste you," she whispered. I didn't reply. She had already taken my cock and had placed the swelled tip of it on her soft lips. Her mouth took me in. I moaned as she drank me up, sucking on me.

My hand found her hair, and I took it strong and firm between my fingers, expressing how *good* she was making me feel. I pulled on her hair. She liked that.

"You're mine," I groaned. She pulled her lips off my cock, saliva dripping from her mouth, and leaned back into her bed.

"Come inside me," she commanded, throwing a condom packet she had in her bedside drawer at me.

And I obeyed.

I wrapped the condom around my shaft and forced myself on her. My engorged cock found her passageway, and I slowly made my way inside her hot, inviting pussy. She gulped as my thick member entered her. I traced my fingers down the length of her body until I found her exposed clit. With her own flowing juices acting as a lubricant, I began to gently circulate her clit with my index finger. Corralling it. Tenderly flicking it. Making her eyes roll to the back of her head.

We were moving in sync. Our bodies seemed to remember each other as if they'd been formed from the same clay. Like they were meant to be together.

I smiled like a wolf as I leaned over her, panting uncontrollably. I was aflame with wild desire. I wanted her completely.

This had been the moment I'd been dreaming about for years. When I was in the desert, surrounded by the sand and the guns and my fellow soldiers, I used to dream about the night Abby and I made sweet love in my bedroom. It had been the best night of my life.

Until now.

I thrust inside her, making Abby moan some more.

Seeing her gorgeous face light up with my cock inside her, seeing her soft lips grow wetter with her own craving for my body, made me even more determined to fuck her relentlessly.

"Fuck me harder," she whispered. I didn't need any more encouragement. I lavished her with attention. My finger worked tirelessly around her sex, and my long cock dug deeper inside her.

It was like a cleansing. Like we were forgiving each other for the past four years in a physical sense. We were doing something no words on a piece of paper could ever express. We were showing our love.

The power that was building between us was overpowering. Strong. Unstoppable.

I knew I was going to come.

I couldn't halt it. Not now. Not after four years of waiting.

This was the moment everything had been leading up to.

I'd missed her, but now I was home.

Abby, sensing how close I was, opened her eyes and bit her lower lip. "Come for me," she commanded. She was close as well. I could sense it.

We both climaxed together.

It was mind-blowing. Everything was taut. Tense.

And then we loosened, and I fell, exhausted, into her arms.

Yep. That four-year wait had been worth it.

36

ABBY

THE FIRST THING I thought about when I woke up was of the broken-down door of my apartment shattered on the floor, leaving my place completely exposed to anyone peeking in.

Gonna need to fix that asap.

The second thought was of Miles, and the fact he was sleeping right next to me in *my bed.*

I turned over and faced the beautiful man lying in my actual freaking bed. I reached up and stroked his sleeping face. So peaceful. So gorgeous.

Last night was *everything.* I was so spontaneously brave in the hallway outside my apartment to just grab him and kiss him like that. I didn't know where that came from inside me. Maybe I'd just been so *exhausted* from all that had happened that I no longer cared. There was a handsome man in front of me and I just had to kiss him.

But what I did know was that it was one of the best decisions I made in my life.

Making love to Miles was more than just sex. It was like a culmination of years of waiting. Years of build-up. It was like my body was homing in on last night. Like everything had been leading up to that moment.

And what a release it was.

I rubbed over the lines of Mile's face with my finger as he lay next to me. His prominent nose. His full lips. His chiseled jaw.

And his scar. It was still there. Just as I remembered it from being a teenager. The same sexy line from some fight he'd been in years ago. A permanent reminder of who he'd been once, frozen in time on his face.

Last night, he was different from that rowdy, rebellious teenager who annoyed me in History class years ago. Last night he'd been strong. Protective. Quick to action. Supportive. Without him, Serenity would be in terrible trouble. Without his quick thinking and physical strength in carrying her the dozen blocks to the hospital, Serenity might not have made it.

He did it all for me.

Miles woke, stirring quickly. His eyes opened and flashed over to me. I smiled at him.

And he smiled back.

"Morning," he said, his voice all croaky from just waking up.

"Morning handsome."

I would do anything for him.

"Had a good sleep?"

"The best."

I thought of Serenity being alone in the hospital. I was suddenly reminded of her, and that made me feel incredibly guilty. Here I was, sleeping in bed with a man whilst she was abandoned in a strange building far away from home.

I moved to get out of bed, but Miles' thick muscular arm wrapped around me, stopping me.

"Where are you going?"

"I need to get to the hospital. I need to see Serenity."

"It's six in the morning," Miles replied. "It's okay. She's probably fast asleep and doesn't want her sister annoying her right now. You heard what she said last night."

I fell back into bed. "I know, but I just feel on edge with her being there, that's all."

"I understand," Miles replied softly. "And so does she. I'm not telling you what you need to do, but I think you should visit her in a few hours, at a more reasonable time. She'll probably appreciate that a lot more than having you barging in when the sun is still rising."

I sighed.

"Yeah. You're probably alright."

"In the meantime," Miles said, lifting himself out of bed and leaning over the side. He pulled up his jeans that had fallen to the floor during our crazy sex session. "I never got the chance to read this. Let me have a look at it."

It took me a moment to grasp what he was talking about, but when it did, I immediately tried to stop him. "Hey, not the letter."

But it was too late. His hand was already in his jean's pocket. He had already taken out the letter.

"Let me read this," he said, pulling it away from my arm's pitiful reach.

"Not in front of me," I cried out, but Miles ignored me. He laughed and unfolded the letter I'd given him the night before, keeping it away from me and my pathetic attempts to snatch it back.

With a smile, he started to read it out loud.

"Dear neighbor. I've just read your letter. Wow. Like you, I also don't know how to start. There's not a lot I can say in response to what you wrote to me. All I can say is, *wow*. There's a lot to take in there. Why you disappeared. Your military tour. You coming back. All the reasons why I thought you had abandoned me, and why you thought I abandoned you. It seems like we've had four years of mismatched communication. Lost communication. Four years lost, when we should've been together. Four years I wish I could retrieve. Four years without you. There's still a lot to process about your letter - I still need to make up my mind about a lot of things in there - but let me tell you one thing I know for sure. *I love you, Miles.* For four years, I've never stopped loving you. From the day you arrived outside my house with your stupid sexy scar to the day you beat up my stepdad all the way to the other day when I first spot you next door. I have always loved you."

Miles took a long pause after he finished reading the letter out loud. I stayed quiet the entire time, feeling strange to hear those words I wrote in the midst of emotion late at night being read back to me in the sobriety of the morning. It was like an alien had written those words, and yet, they were speaking the truth. My truth.

Miles lowered the piece of paper and slowly turned to me. All I could see were his blue eyes.

"I love you, Abby."

That was all he said. It was all that was said for a very long time as we lay there in silence. We stared at each other for an eternity.

It was like we were reunited. Like we had been transported from that night four years ago when we first had sex into the present day.

Like nothing had changed between us.

After the long pause, I finally spoke.

"I love you, Miles."

"We've found each other," he said. "And maybe we can start again."

"Maybe we can."

He leaned back into bed and sighed as if he was deflating. I was still sat up, completely shocked. The events of the last twenty-four hours seemed to be a dream. From a nightmare with Serenity's seizure to a dream with Miles admitting he loved me. So much had changed.

Miles spoke again, his voice tiny. "I've been thinking..."

"Oh yeah, what about?"

"I've saved a lot of money from being in the Army," he said. "I haven't spent much in the last few years."

"What do you mean?"

What's he saying?

"We can use that money I've saved up so that you don't have to work. I can work instead. You can go to college."

"What are you talking about?"

"The future, Abby. I'm talking about the future. What we can do together."

"You want to pay for me to go to college?" I asked in disbelief.

I can't have him doing that.

"No. Not you. I'm saying I can pay for Serenity," he replied. "I can help get her the education she needs. I was giving it a think last night. We've lost four years, and I want to do something that'll change things. With her stuff paid for, it means that you don't have to work at that Irish bar anymore. It means that you can spend more time with her and maybe you can pursue education part-time. I can work instead. You were always the smarter one out of the both of us. You were my History tutor after all. You should be in education. You shouldn't waste your life. And besides, I have some contacts from my Army days who've offered me jobs here in the city. I can work one of those and support us."

It took me a few seconds to process what he was saying.

"You're going to pay for Serenity? I won't have to work? I can go to college? You're going to support us?"

"That's what I'm saying," he replied.

"Why?" I asked. "Why would you do that for us?"

"Because, Abby." He faced me again. "Because I love you."

EPILOGUE

DEAR NEIGHBOR,

I DON'T KNOW *why I'm writing this when I am sitting in bed next to you. I mean, you are literally right beside me. I could just speak these words instead of putting them to paper. But, in some strange way, I reckon it's better to write them down. Maybe we could keep these words as proof that all this has happened, or something? Prosperity and all that.*

So.

Where to start?

It's been a year since Serenity's seizure, a year since you ran all the way to the hospital with her in your arms. A whole year since we made love in my broken-in apartment. Thanks for fixing the door, by the way.

It's been the best year of my life since then.

You stayed true to your word, didn't you? You paid for me to leave that bar job, and you took up an offer from one of your Army pals. Curtis. You saved his life out there overseas, and then he offered you a good job back home. A job that covered both Serenity and me as well. I was able to devote my time to both helping Serenity recover from the seizure and to her education, and also on my own part-time studies. I went into nursing to help other girls like Serenity. I never knew that was my passion in life. Maybe you did. You were the one to encourage me into pursuing it after all. Sneaky you.

And then you took us on holiday. We traveled to Europe. We went to the non-combat zones where you were deployed over there. You showed me the hospital in Germany where Curtis was treated. You showed me the bars in Amsterdam you once spent a drunken night out with your unit on leave. And then you showed me London. You took me to the top of the tallest building there. The Shard. We looked out over the view from the top of the skyscraper, and then you kneeled down, pulled out a ring, and proposed to me.

And I said yes.

Of course, you know all this. You were right there.

It really has been the best year of my life, enough to make up for the four that preceded it.

You, Serenity, and I are a family. The family we created from the ashes of our old toxic ones.

And I can't wait to see what the future brings.

I think this will be the last letter I'll ever write to you because you're no longer my neighbor. You're now my fiancé.

And there's no point in these anymore. There's no need to write secret letters to each other now that we live under the same roof.

We have each other now.

So. This is it.

Goodbye.

And hello to a new chapter in our lives.

Love,
 Your Neighbor

ABOUT THE AUTHOR

Rebecca has had the storytelling bug since... forever!

What Rebecca likes most is writing steamy hot filthy romances with sweet happy endings sprinkled with some delicious bad boys.

Born and raised in an Aussie coastal town, she loves travelling around the world - meeting new people and discovering their stories.

Aside from adventuring she also enjoys a good rainy day in with a good book or at a hot beach catching the sun.

She's a world-class napping professional. You'll most likely find her asleep snuggled up on a sofa somewhere cozy.

For other titles and information please visit
rebeccacastle.com

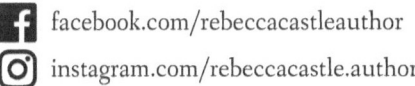 facebook.com/rebeccacastleauthor
instagram.com/rebeccacastle.author